PREVIEW HARVEY

ALSO BY BRUCE KIMMEL

The Kritzer trilogy:
Benjamin Kritzer
Kritzerland
Kritzer Time

Writer's Block
Rewind
How to Write a Dirty Book
Red Gold
Patrick Bronstein Presents
Thrill Ride
GEE
Some Days Are Murder
'Tis the Season to be Murdered

Adriana Hofstetter mysteries:
Murder at Hollywood High
Murder at the Grove
Murder at the Hollywood Historical Society
Murder at the Masquers
Murder at the School Musical
Murder at the Hollywood Division
Murder at the Magic Castle

There's Mel, There's Woody, and There's You (memoir)
Album Produced By... (memoir)
Simply: A Lifetime of Lyrics

PREVIEW HARVEY

A Novel by

Bruce Kimmel

authorHOUSE®

AuthorHouse™
1663 Liberty Drive
Bloomington, IN 47403
www.authorhouse.com
Phone: 833-262-8899

Published by AuthorHouse 04/27/2023

ISBN: 979-8-8230-0639-2 (sc)
ISBN: 979-8-8230-0640-8 (hc)
ISBN: 979-8-8230-0638-5 (e)

Print information available on the last page.

Cover design by Doug Haverty
Cover photograph courtesy by Bison Archives

For all the preview nuts I've known, and for my beautiful,
wonderful, warm, and hilarious
Cindy Williams

FOREWORD

It's funny what you don't know. I'm a child of the '90s and I say that with some embarrassment. Born in 1996, so if you're doing the math, at the time of writing this in 2023, I just turned twenty-seven.

I have never felt part of my generation. I don't sit around and nostalgically pine for the movies of my youth like most do. I had little use for them then and even less use for them now. Maybe it was my mother's influence on me, but I grew up loving the classics—classic movies, classic rock and roll, classic singers, classic jazz, classic big band or rhythm and blues, classic literature, classic TV shows—you know, the classics. The music of my generation either gives me a headache or puts me to sleep. The stuff that passes for literature today puts me to sleep.

I'm not a gamer, I'm not a computer whiz, I don't live on my cellphone, I don't text relentlessly, I'm not on Twitter or TikTok. I'll admit to a Facebook and Instagram account, but that's all you're getting out of me. So, in school I guess I was kind of an oddball. Thankfully, I had a good sense of humor, always, and while I suppose I was bullied a bit, I never let it get to me. I never smoked, did drugs, none of the stuff others were doing. I'm sure there are those who are reading this now, thinking, "What a moron" and I'm fine with that–in fact, I wouldn't have it any other way. I have a few friends who understand who I am and who enjoy my generational peculiarities and we all get along fine and laugh about things and have a pretty good perspective on the world in which we live. I also write in cursive and if people can't read it, not my problem.

Where is all this leading, this preamble? Well, let me get right to that because it's the point of what you're about to read. My mother's mother had a sister who had a son, a peculiar sort, only of a completely different era. And last year, she thought it was time to give me something that my mother's mother's sister had given her, a box of cassette tapes that she'd found when her son passed away, sitting in a corner of what she described as a very small, very cluttered studio apartment he'd lived in for decades.

First of all, I had to go on eBay and find a working cassette deck. There were a lot of them, so I searched on Google to see which were the best. Yes, I use Google and the Internet, so I guess that makes me at least somewhat modern. I bought the best of what I found on eBay, a Technics RS-B905, which the seller described as a top-of-the-line player that was "minty fresh" in box, like new. It was listed at $240 but had a make-an-offer option, so I made an offer of $200, and the seller accepted it. A week later, I had the machine. I began listening. Each cassette was numbered and dated, so I began at the beginning.

And what I heard was so fascinating, my distant cousin talking about his life, from start to finish. It was like entering a completely different universe or world, a time capsule of the past and mostly to do with movies and something I'd never even heard of—major studio previews. I Googled it and could find nothing about it. But I didn't have to because on these cassettes was the story of a life, an obsessive-compulsive life, lived in movie theaters that showed major studio previews. As I'd come to learn, major studio previews were movies that hadn't come out yet, but were shown to the public in advance, sometimes in finished form, sometimes in unfinished form. And no one had any idea what movie they'd be seeing.

Audiences would sometimes fill out preview cards saying what they thought of the movie they'd just seen. I began to read up on several famous previews that hadn't gone well: *The Magnificent Ambersons*, *Chinatown*, and others, from the 1940s to the 1970s.

I was fascinated by his voice, his way of talking, but most of all his obsession, the major studio preview. Although he would never say it, listening to the tapes it becomes apparent that he was a legendary figure, a real character, as they say. The studios adopted him—he was a good luck charm to them. Well, I don't want to give any more away, as no one can present this story better than the person telling it, a person who became known as Preview Harvey.

I made no attempt to edit the cassettes. I transcribed them word for word and present them with no commentary because none is needed. It's a life told in stream of consciousness ramblings and reminiscences, and being stream of consciousness, I have tried not to over-punctuate—you won't find any colons or semicolons, only periods and commas, and in terms of commas, only when I thought they were completely necessary for understanding what he was saying. He didn't talk in commas or semicolons or colons, and I wanted the reader to hear the flow of his talking because it is part of who he was. Well, you'll see.

I also apologize in advance for the length of some of the paragraphs, but that's the way he talks, jumping and flipping from thing to thing like a ten-year-old on a trampoline.

I think there is some worth, some value in putting this out in the ether. It was a time we're never going to have again. A unique time lived by a unique person. And so, without further comment, I give you, in his own words, Preview Harvey.

Nicholas Grayson
Ladera Ranch, California
March 2023

CASSETTE ONE

Testing. Testing.

Okay, okay, let's see if this works, hold on a minute. Okay, so it works, so let me tell you, let me tell you something, I got a new thing a new thing it's a tape recorder thing, but a new kind not a reel-to-reel kind and they call it a, a cassette recorder. It's portable and you don't have reels like the old recorders, this has the tape in a little thing like a little plastic shell thing, I guess that's the cassette and you just pop it in, you pop it in and push play and record at the same time and I'm making a recording on it now, it's recording and I'm talking and that goes on this cassette thing, thirty minutes a side, it says so, I can talk for thirty minutes at once on one side, flip it over, and talk for another thirty minutes, but I don't have to talk for thirty minutes, see, that's the thing, I can stop and start and record whenever I want to. There, see I stopped and I started and I love this thing already, this Panasonic thing cassette recorder thing because you don't have to put the tape through those gizmos which I always did wrong anyway and sometimes the tape would come off the reels like spaghetti and that wasn't fun.

Anyway, anyway, why am I doing this, making tapes of me talking about, well, you know, talking about, you know, my life, my life so far, so, why am I doing this? I don't know, I just, I just, I just felt like I needed to do it, to do this, to do this thing, to put my life on little plastic cassette tapes, so if anyone ever played them, like I don't know who that would be, but let's say if anyone played them they'd know I existed, that I was a person, a guy they called Preview Harvey. Even if no one listens to these, at least I made a record, well, not a record, a cassette thing, at least I made a cassette tape thing of how it was and how it is, for me, for Preview Harvey. Oh, and I guess I should say, I guess I should say it's, it's 1968 when I'm making this, when I'm making this, this record of things on cassette tapes.

I gotta say something right away, I have to say something before I really start, before I really start I have to say something right away. I have a condition, some kind of condition. I don't know the name of it, maybe there isn't a name for it, maybe it's just a condition. My parents, see, my parents, they didn't know what to do about the condition, I mean, they knew I had some kind of something, so they took me to a couple of doctors but the doctors didn't know what my condition was, they knew something was going on but they didn't know a name for it, there wasn't a name they knew for it, for whatever was going on. See, the condition was, the condition I had was, well, still is, I still have whatever it was and still is, I'll always have it, well, the condition thing is that I get fixated on something and I repeat it over and over again, I repeat all the time even when something somewhere in the back of my brain is saying you're repeating again, I still repeat because I get fixated on something and can't get off whatever it is that I'm fixated on and I'm fixated on different things at different times and then I repeat things and I guess that's confusing for people who don't get that I have a condition, and it's probably annoying too, well, I know it's annoying because I repeat things and people don't like it and it's probably why I don't have any friends, never really had any friends, girls or boys, never had friends like other people had friends. I had my dog, Clara, Clara was my friend and Clara didn't care that I repeated things and fixated on things, Clara only cared if I scratched her stomach, in fact, you could say Clara had a condition too, like she was, you know, she was like fixated on having her stomach scratched, she could just have me do that forever and I knew that because she would just lay on her back with her paws in the air, just lay like that until I scratched her stomach and if I'd never scratched her stomach she probably would have, she probably would have just laid there in that position until she died and they took her away to the dead animal place. I know this because she did die and she was in that position when she died and they took her to the dead animal place. That was a sad day when Clara died in that position. When I die, that's the way I want to go, you know, on my back, arms and feet in the air, waiting for someone to scratch my stomach.

Anyway, my parents, Earl and Mellie, short for Melanie, they knew I had a condition and that the doctors didn't have a name for it so they gave it a name, they gave my condition a name, they called it That's Just Harvey. That was the name of my condition. I liked it and I still like it. That's Just Harvey.

But see, I do this all the time, I do this all the time, I get ahead of myself, that's what I do. I don't want to get ahead of myself but it just happens, getting ahead of myself. So, before anyone knew I had the That's Just Harvey condition, I was born. Mother told me it was at 6:15 in the morning. She said that was a god-awful time to have a baby but that's when I decided I was coming out and there was no, you know, there was no stopping me and out I came and mother told me it was so painful, my coming out of her was so painful that she thought she was going to die or using her favorite expression that she was going to eat the head of a chicken. See, she, you know, see, she used that expression all the time and I had nightmares about eating the head of a chicken for my entire childhood. Anyway, I was born, she didn't die or eat the head of a chicken, and I eventually walked and talked.

She called me her little person, that was her nickname for me, that's what she called me all the time. Look, it's my little person, she'd say, that's what she'd say and I think, this is just what I think, I don't know if it's a fact or anything, but I think her calling me that twenty times a day insured that I would be a short person when I grew up and that's what happened, I mean, father was only 5'6" and mother was 4'9" and I landed in the middle at 5'3" barely, I mean almost, not quite, almost 5'3", which is how tall I am not that you can use the word tall, that's how small I am is more like it. You know, you know how they, how people sometimes say, you know, they say something like, I want someone I can look up to? You know how they say that, well, I had to look up to everyone because mostly everyone was taller than me. My little person. She could've just, she could've just said, my person or my boy or just said look how big my boy is getting.

Maybe if we'd prayed to God to make me be at least as tall as father, maybe if we'd prayed to God then I might have been taller, if, you know, if God actually listens when people pray. But you have to be, you have to be religious or something, right, you have to be religious or something and my parents could never make up their minds about which religion they wanted to be. I mean, I mean, I mean we were Lutheran then they decided we were Presbyterian then Protestant and then Episcopalian, you know, I didn't, I didn't understand any of it, it all sounded the same to me. And then, and then, my parents decided we were atheists so what was the point of praying since we were atheists and there was no God listening to prayers and here I am at almost 5'3" small, my mother's little person.

If you haven't figured it out already, I talk very fast, I've always talked very fast, faster than a speeding bullet like they said on *Superman*. So, mother not only called me, she not only called me my little person, she called me my little motormouth too. I guess I think of things so fast that I have to talk fast to, you know, I have to talk fast to keep up with my thoughts.

I suppose I should say my name is Harvey, Harvey Minton, that's what my name is just to get that on the, you know, just to get that on the record, Harvey Minton. Mother always pronounced my name, she pronounced my name Hahveeeeee, that's how my mother would pronounce my name, Hahveeeeee with no "r" sound, like she was from Boston or something, but she wasn't from Boston she was from Chicago originally but they moved a lot, my parents moved a lot before they settled in Los Angeles and had me which if I didn't mention it, I don't think I mentioned it so I'll mention it now, they had me in 1940, that's the year when she told me I popped out of her and she thought she was going to die or eat the head of a chicken.

Father, see, father, father was, I asked him one day, I was four or five, I asked him one day what do you do, I mean, what's your job? He said a welder, that was his job. I asked him what's a welder, what do welders do and he said weld. I asked if I could come to work with him so I could see him weld and he said they don't allow kids near welders because it's dangerous. I told him I'm a kid and I'm near a welder and I'm not in danger. He said, I'm not welding now, if I was welding now you couldn't be here because you're a kid and it's dangerous.

When I was little, well, I mean I'm still little but when I was a kid, when I was a kid, when I was little, I loved coloring books, my room was filled with, you know, my room was filled with coloring books because I loved them and crayons, I loved crayons and coloring in my coloring books with crayons from my big, my big box of crayons. I guess I should say that I colored outside the lines. My parents didn't like it that I colored outside the lines and didn't make pretty coloring book pictures but the thing is, the thing is, I thought they were pretty. Why does everything have to be in the lines? Who made that rule? Who makes any rule? I still have them, all my coloring books they're in a, you know, they're in a, in a box in the closet in my apartment, the apartment I live in, where I live, but I don't want to talk about the apartment yet because I'm talking about, I'm talking about when I was little, a kid, and in my apartment I'm not a kid anymore.

My parents, you know, my parents that I was talking about, my parents loved magazines. They came in the mail, the magazines came in the mail because they had subscriptions to *Life*, *Look*, *The Saturday Evening Post*, *National Geographic*, *Time*, and *Saturday Review*. Whatever the, whatever the current issues were they were laid out on the coffee table. They loved, they loved having all the magazines on the coffee table, the current issues, but they never read them, never even opened them, they just liked them on the coffee table. Sometimes I'd look at the pictures in them but mother would get very upset with me if I didn't put them back the way they were, you know, if I didn't put them back perfectly placed like they were, that would really upset her if they weren't perfectly placed like they were. They never threw them out either, the magazines, they kept them in bundles, in bundles in closets.

Other than coloring books, my favorite things were board games, especially Monopoly and Sorry, but all board games and we had lots of board games. Mother and father didn't like playing board games with me because I always won even when I was six because I could, I could fixate, that's what she called it, fixating, I could fixate on the game and think fast and so I won and they didn't like that but I did.

I liked playing the ones I didn't understand too, like Camelot, that was a fun game that I didn't understand, but mother thought that was stupid playing board games you didn't understand but I played them anyway because that was fun, at least for me. My sister loved board games too and we played them together. Oh yeah, I had a sister, I guess I should mention that I had a sister, sorry for jumping all over the place but that's how it works with my brain, mother always said my brain was like a Mexican jumping bean. Anyway, I had a sister, Pearl was her name, my sister Pearl. She popped out of mother when I was four. My mother had gained a lot of weight and that's because Pearl was inside her waiting to pop out.

Pearl was a good baby and she was my friend, Pearl was my friend and we played board games, we played board games when she was four and five and we listened to *Boston Blackie* on the radio and we laughed all the time and she was pretty and funny. I can't talk about it anymore, I get sad because I miss her, she didn't have my condition she didn't have a condition at all, she just got sick and died and I miss her and her smile and she didn't care that I colored outside the lines.

I'm stopping now.

Okay, okay, I'm back, okay I'm back, I had to stop because I get sad about Pearl. So anyway, so anyway, where was I? It doesn't matter, my brain is like a Mexican jumping bean, that's what mother always told me. I went to school, grammar school first and that wasn't easy, grammar school, because I had That's Just Harvey, my condition, and the kids at school made fun of me because I wasn't like them and I had That's Just Harvey and they didn't understand why I wasn't like them so they made fun of me and I didn't have any friends at school because everyone made fun of me. I did have a friend but not in grammar school but I'll talk about my friend later because that wasn't in grammar school. What I want to talk about, what I want to talk about, what got me through everything was the movies. That's what I want to talk about right now, the movies because that's what got me through everything, that's how I, that's how I became who I am, I mean, I'm not that complicated, but the movies were my friends from the very first time I saw one.

I was five when mother and father took me to my first movie, I was five and I remember it like it just happened, like it was just the other day or something even though it wasn't just the other day, it was a long time ago. Pearl had to stay home with a sitter because she was, she was, she was too young to go to the movies or anywhere really. But I was five and they took me to a movie theater on Hollywood Boulevard, oh wait, I didn't talk about where we lived yet and I should talk about that just so I make a record of it on this cassette thing. We lived in the Gaylord Apartments building on Wilshire, that's where we lived, a two-bedroom apartment on the fourth floor of the Gaylord Apartments building on Wilshire, apartment 402. We moved from there a few years later but I'll talk about that later so I don't jump around too much like a Mexican jumping bean. I'm just trying to make a record of my, you know, my, when I was younger and how it all began, but there I go again getting off the track because I'm a motormouth and mother also said I was yakky, endlessly yakky.

Anyway, when I was five we got in the car and drove up to Hollywood Boulevard. I'd never been that far away, that far away from the Gaylord Apartments. My parents said we were going to the movies, to see a movie in a movie theater and I didn't know what that meant, I didn't know what a movie was or a movie theater or Hollywood Boulevard. I was five, I only knew about coloring books and board games and *Boston Blackie* on the radio, that's all I knew.

Anyway, we went in the car to Hollywood Boulevard to a movie theater called the Paramount to see a movie called *Hold That Blonde*. I was, I was, I didn't know what to expect or what I was in for. There were colorful posters in windows outside the Paramount, there were all these posters, colorful posters, and father told me they were for movies, like what we were going to see and the one in front of us was *Hold That Blonde*. We went inside and it was, it was, we went inside and it was like being in a new world it was so big and beautiful, like a palace or something, with beautiful rugs and walls and a place where they sold candy and popcorn. I didn't know what popcorn was but I knew, I knew what candy was and I loved candy and mother bought me some Tootsie Rolls and she got a new kind of candy, a new kind of candy called Dots and she let me try a couple, I tried a couple and I liked them, I liked the Dots because they were chewy and gooey and got in my teeth and I liked them better than Tootsie Rolls because Tootsie Rolls were just brown and Dots were different colors, and mother practically let me eat the whole box of Dots during the movie.

The inside, the inside where they actually showed the movie even though I didn't know what a movie was, the inside was even more beautiful than what mother called the, the lobby, where she bought the Tootsie Rolls and Dots and a Coca-Cola in a cup not a bottle like we had at home, bottles of Coca-Cola. We sat down and I looked at the beautiful curtains and mother said the movie screen was behind those beautiful curtains, but I could have, I could have just watched those beautiful curtains.

Then the lights went down, they went down or off and the beautiful curtains opened and I couldn't believe, I couldn't believe what I was seeing, this thing called, this thing called a movie. There was writing and it kept changing. I was a, I was a pretty good, a pretty good reader by then and I could read names and other stuff I didn't understand like director and starring and costumes.

Then there were, there were, then there were people on the screen and it was so funny, the people on the screen were doing and saying funny things and the people in the theater were laughing. I didn't really understand what was going on on the screen but I was laughing, I was laughing too because other people were laughing and I wanted to laugh too. The man in it had a funny face and did funny things, and I couldn't take my eyes off the lady in it, I couldn't take my eyes off her because she was, she was the prettiest thing I'd ever seen.

After the movie was over I knew what a movie was. On the way home, father told me there were movies in color too and I asked him, I said what's the pretty lady's name because I wanted to marry her and he said, he said her name was, her name was Veronica Lake and I loved her and wanted to marry her. That was my first movie and then I went to the movies all the time after that, all the time, whenever I could, not just to the big theaters like the Paramount, but to smaller theaters near where we lived at the Gaylord Apartments. I wanted to,

I wanted to live, to live in the movie theaters. Anyway, that was my first movie and I saw it on TV a year ago, I saw it on TV a year ago and it wasn't funny at all, but Veronica Lake was, she was, Veronica Lake was still the most beautiful lady I've ever seen.

That was the start, that was the start, the beginning of it all but not the most important part, I'm getting to the most important part, because that's what all this has been leading to, the important part, that's where all this has been leading to.

After grammar school, after grammar school, I, I, I went to junior high school and remember how I said I didn't have any friends in grammar school, well, I didn't have any friends in junior high school either because they thought I was an oddball, that's what they called me, an oddball, and they made, they made fun of me like grammar school, and I just tried to stay away from everyone, even though a couple of mean boys said if I wasn't careful they'd kill me, they'd kill me because they didn't like oddballs in their school.

Anyway, I know I'm rambling but that's part of That's Just Harvey, I ramble, I'm yakky, I can't help it, but let me tell you about my one friend in junior high school who I met in social studies, her name was Joyce, Joyce Aronovitz, that was her name, Joyce Aronovitz. She was nice and sometimes we even went to the movies together because she was nice and thought I was funny even though I didn't think I was funny and I thought she was nice, with a nice smile and always, she was always smiling and happy and seemed full of life and joy. I told her that, I told her she was full of life and joy and that she even, that she even had joy in her name Joyce and she thought that was pretty funny, she thought that was funny and said ha and that I had ha in Harvey and I thought that was funny, ha in Harvey. She didn't care about That's Just

Harvey, my condition and I didn't have to worry about her wanting to kill me like the, like the mean boys.

We weren't friends that long though, we weren't friends that long though because we moved from the Gaylord Apartments to fake Beverly Hills, fake because, I mean, we were close to Beverly Hills but weren't really Beverly Hills because we were close but still were in Los Angeles. We moved to a four-unit building, a four-unit building, which was better than an apartment in the Gaylord Apartments because a four-unit building was almost, was almost like a, more like a house than an apartment. Our fake Beverly Hills almost house was on Rexford just south of Whitworth and if we'd been, if we'd been one block north of Whitworth we would have been real Beverly Hills but we weren't, we were fake Beverly Hills because we were south of Whitworth. I liked our new almost house much better than the Gaylord Apartments, which always smelled bad because you could smell what people, what people were cooking and they were cooking, they were cooking all different things and it smelled bad but the new almost house didn't smell bad because you couldn't smell what people were cooking.

Anyway, I didn't stay in touch with Joyce and she didn't stay in touch with me and I was in a new school, a new school that was like the old school in that they made fun of me and thought I was an oddball although they didn't use that exact word, they just didn't like me and I went back to having no friends, not even one friend like Joyce. But at least I had new movie theaters to go to in real Beverly Hills and they were really nice big ones and I went, I went all the time.

And then, now I'm going to tell you what happened because it, I'm going to tell you what happened one day because it was going to change my, you know, it was going to change my life forever. I'm going to tell you what happened now. I can't even tell you why it happened, not really, it was just one of those things, like that song mother sang all the time, it was just one of those things. It was April 6, 1954, that's when it was just one of those things happened, April 6, 1954 when I was fourteen years old. I was looking at the newspaper to see what movie, what movie I might like to, I might like to see in real Beverly Hills, when I saw something in the newspaper. I'd seen it before but I'd, I'd, I'd never, I'd never paid attention to it, but now I saw it and it just took hold of me, I don't know how to describe it, it just grabbed, it just grabbed my attention and took hold of me. I didn't, I didn't, you know, I didn't know what it meant even, but it grabbed my attention and took hold of me and I guess because of my That's Just Harvey condition I became fixated on it like I did with board games, that's just part of That's Just Harvey, my condition, I become fixated on things and that's it, I'm fixated on them forever, I can't help it, it's just one of those things like the song.

Anyway, what grabbed me and took hold of me, what I became fixated on were four words, even though the fourth word wasn't important it was the first three words that were important and that I fixated on, that grabbed my attention and took hold of me and wouldn't let go, even though I'd seen them before. For me, those three words, those three words became the most magical, the most magical words I'd ever heard and really the most magical words in the English language. Just those three words, Major Studio Preview, with the fourth word always being Tonight! I was hypnotized by Major Studio Preview even though as I said already I didn't know what that meant.

I immediately went to mother and told her, I told her I had to go to the Major Studio Preview Tonight and I showed her where it said that in the paper, above the, above the listing for Fox West Coast Theaters. She looked at it and read it aloud,

Major Studio Preview Tonight in Cinemascope and color. I told her I had to go see whatever that was and she told me that a preview was a movie that hadn't come out yet, a preview of the entire movie that only that audience would see until the movie came out.

That made me, that made me, I was hooked even more, especially because it was, it was, you know, in Cinemascope and I'd never seen anything in Cinemascope yet, I only had seen the ads for *The Robe* and the ad for *The Robe* said The First Motion Picture in Cinemascope, The Modern Miracle You See Without Glasses. I didn't wear glasses anyway, but I wanted to see The Modern Miracle You See Without Glasses more than anything even if it's a movie about a robe, like my bathrobe. But I hadn't seen it yet, I hadn't seen The Modern Miracle You See Without Glasses. This was my chance to not only see a Major Studio Preview but Cinemascope and color too. Mother knew me well enough, she knew me well enough to know that there would be, there would be, she wouldn't be able to talk me out of going so she told father we were going and we should get there for the movie that was playing there so we'd have good seats.

The Major Studio Preview was at a theater I'd never been to in Westwood. I'd never been to Westwood, but I'd heard of Westwood because of the movie section in the paper. The theater we were going to was called, it was called the Village and I had no idea, I had no idea that the Village was going to become so important to me but there I go again jumping around like a Mexican jumping bean.

The Major Studio Preview was at 8:30, so we ate dinner early and drove to Westwood at 5:30, with father complaining, you know, complaining the entire time that gas had gone up to twenty-nine cents a gallon and we weren't made of money, you know, because he was always complaining about money and how much things cost, it was almost like he had a condition, like That's Just Earl, but his condition wasn't like my condition, his condition was about money and not ending up in the poorhouse.

I know, I know, I'm going on and on but that's what I do, go on and on and on and there's nothing I can do about it, just in case anyone ever, just in case anyone ever hears this cassette tape. So, anyway, we got to the Village Theater and went in, with father complaining about the cost of the, you know, about the cost of the tickets.

It was a very nice theater but not exactly the Paramount or any of the other, you know, any of the other movie palaces I'd gone to by then. We found seats even though it was already pretty crowded, and we saw the movie that was playing there then, we saw the movie that was playing there then, called *Roman Holiday* and it was in black-and-white and was good and I liked the girl in it, I liked her but not like I liked Veronica Lake, and the girl's name was Audrey Hepburn and I liked her better later but that's later and this was April 6, 1954. Even though I, even though I enjoyed *Roman Holiday*, I couldn't wait for the Major Studio Preview, I couldn't wait, I couldn't wait to see what it was, what movie it was in Cinemascope and color.

I know, I know, I just keep going on and on about this because even right this minute I can, I can, I can remember the, you know, I can remember the excitement of it all, the excitement of the lights going down and then the curtains parting and parting and parting and parting and the Cinemascope screen, which was so wide and long and the hush, the hush in the theater as everyone waited to see what the Major Studio Preview was.

The first thing, the first thing we saw was WB, which meant Warner Bros. and I knew that because I'd already seen a lot of movies with the WB thing at the, you know, at the beginning. But this WB thing was in, was in Cinemascope and it was so wide it really was like a, like a Modern Miracle, and then it said A Cinemascope Production and the music was so loud and coming from all over the theater like nothing I'd ever heard, I'd never heard anything, anything like that, and then the title of the movie came on, *The High and the Mighty* was the title and some people went ooh and ahh and then it said starring John Wayne and the whole audience applauded, the whole audience applauded and I applauded too because they were, but also because, you know, also because I loved John Wayne movies and this one was in Cinemascope and color.

All I can tell you is, all I can tell you is I loved every second of this Major Studio Preview. It was so exciting in Cinemascope, so wide, and the music was so loud and John Wayne whistled and saved the day, saved the day and the airplane that was going to crash even though everyone called him an ancient pelican, he still saved the day and the airplane that was going to crash and at the end after he's saved the airplane he went off at the end whistling and I knew, I just knew, I knew I had to see every Major Studio Preview I could, which got confusing and I'll tell you why it got confusing in a minute, but it did, it got confusing and I'll tell you why in a minute.

I motormouthed and was yakky all the way home and it was late by the time we got home and mother told me I had to brush my teeth and get to bed because I had school in the morning, I had school in the morning and I didn't want to go, I wanted to think about Cinemascope and John Wayne whistling and saving the airplane even though he was an ancient pelican. All I knew was, all I knew was I couldn't wait for *The High and the Mighty* to come out so I could see it again and again and I couldn't wait until my next Major

Studio Preview and I'll talk about that after I eat some soup because I'm hungry and I feel like soup, Campbell's chicken noodle soup, my favorite soup that I eat practically every day, Campbell's chicken noodle soup.

Okay, so soup was good like it always is, Campbell's chicken noodle soup. I also want to say, I just want to say that I love, I love this cassette thing, it's like, it's like getting in a time machine, all this remembering things I haven't thought about in I don't know, I don't know how long and I haven't thought about these things and it's fun to just, fun to just be a motormouth and yakky and remember all these things, these things that, I don't know, these things that made me whoever me is and that's why I love this cassette thing.

Now I can talk about my second preview but first I want to say that I was fixated on *The High and the Mighty* and couldn't think of anything else until it finally opened on May 27th at the Egyptian in Hollywood. I just want to say, well, I made mother and father take me there that weekend, and they didn't want to see it again so they went across the street to the Vogue, the Vogue Theater, to see *Elephant Walk*. I didn't have, I didn't have too much interest in seeing an elephant walk, and it wasn't in Cinemascope anyway and I only, you know, I only wanted to see Cinemascope.

The Egyptian was beautiful, a real palace like the Paramount and when the curtains parted and parted even wider than the Village, Cinemascope was even more of a Modern Miracle than it was at the Village and the sound was even louder and coming from everywhere, all over the theater. Anyway, I loved it even more the second time, you know, I loved it and John Wayne and all the colorful characters and the saving the, you know, the saving the airplane from crashing and then John Wayne walking off at the end whistling. So,

I was, I was, so I was fixated on the whistling, the thing John Wayne was whistling, you know, the music he was whistling.

When mother and father picked me up I told them I was fixated on the music, the whistling, and they knew what that meant when I was fixated they knew what that meant so father drove over to Wallichs Music City close by, he drove over there and we all went in and we were lucky well I was lucky they had a record of that music, a record, a 78 on Coral Records with a pretty orange label that said Theme from *The High and the Mighty*, Dimitri Tiomkin and his Orchestra. Mother saw the look in my, you know, she saw the look in my eyes and told father he'd better buy it or that's all they'd hear about from now until kingdom come.

I played the record when I got home, I played it when I got home and it never left the record player because I played it every day and every night and I whistled like John Wayne. Then the movie came to the Picwood Theater in Westwood and that was close to us, that was so close that I could take a bus on Pico and get there in ten minutes, it was so close to us. I saw it twelve more times at the Picwood because it was so close to us and it played there for three weeks and I saw it twelve times because, you know, That's Just Harvey.

Oh yeah, I want to, I want to tell about my second preview but I, but I, but I also want to tell you why it was so confusing with seeing Major Studio Previews sometimes, that's what I wanted to talk about. So, it was confusing because sometimes, sometimes there were four or five Major Studio Previews in one night and how were you, how were you supposed to, you know, how were you supposed to choose which one to go to? They were all over town and how were you supposed to choose? That's what was confusing but I decided that if there was more than, if there was more than one Major Studio Preview I'd choose the best theater and see that one. Anyway, I just wanted to say that that's why it was confusing.

But I want to talk about my second preview, because I, because I learned something, I learned something important with my second preview. It was October 21, 1954 and I was, I'd been, I was desperate to see another Major Studio Preview, but I hadn't seen one since the first one because I was, because I was so busy seeing *The High and the Mighty* and we weren't made out of money.

Anyway, anyway, I was looking in the movie section, it was a Thursday night, I remember it was a Thursday night because I remember everything from back then, I remember everything because I don't know why. There were no Major Studio Previews anywhere that I could see. Usually, usually it, it mentioned the preview above the Fox West Coast Theaters or above the ads for the, above the ads for the movies.

So, I was looking, I was looking to see if any Major Studio Previews were listed, if they were just listed in the theater listing, you know, where they listed the theaters and in the Independent Theaters I found one, I found one in the Independent Theaters listing at the Baldwin Theater. I didn't know the Baldwin Theater, and the listing said La Brea and Rodeo. That was confusing because we had a real Beverly Hills Rodeo near us, but La Brea wasn't near us so I didn't, I didn't understand La Brea and Rodeo, fake Rodeo like fake Beverly Hills.

The theater listing said Studio Feature Preview and not Major Studio Preview and that was confusing, that was confusing too, like two Rodeos, one in real Beverly Hills and one somewhere, somewhere on La Brea. But I got it into my mind that I wanted to see what a Studio Feature Preview was so I told mother I'd like to see the Studio Feature Preview at the Baldwin and she laughed and said, she laughed and called me incorrigible. That was better, I thought that was better, that was better than motormouth or yakky. So, she called father at his welding place, where he welded, his welding place, and told him and he said we, you know, we weren't made out of money.

When he came home he saw the look in my eyes and so we got in the car, we all got in the car and drove to the Baldwin on La Brea and fake Rodeo. It took about thirty minutes, about thirty minutes, it took about thirty minutes to get there and I'd never seen that area before and I, well, I'd never seen a movie theater that looked like the Baldwin on La Brea and fake Rodeo, I'd never seen a theater like that.

I wish, I wish I could, I wish I could show you a picture of the Baldwin but this is a cassette and so I can't, I can't show you a picture of the Baldwin. I was only there that, that one, that one time but I can describe it to you because I remember everything. It was not near anything, I mean, it wasn't next to any buildings, it was just there, it was just there by itself. It looked like, well, like something out of the future or something like that, with a long marquee and two big half-circle things, like arches or something.

The marquee said *Duel in the Sun* and Studio Feature Preview Tonite, and I'd never seen tonight spelled like tonite with an, an I-T-E so that was confusing and I was already, I was already confused enough as it was from all the other things that were confusing.

We went in and found seats, we found seats about halfway down and watched the end of *Duel in the Sun* but I didn't know what it was about because we only saw the end and so I didn't know what it was about. After The End, the lights came up and the curtains closed. I looked up, I looked up at the ceiling and it was like a half circle, like a half circle too, I don't know if I'm, if I'm describing it right, it was like we were in a spaceship like in *The Day the Earth Stood Still*, which I saw in 1951 at the Wilshire Theater, a beautiful theater that wasn't, that wasn't too far from us on Rexford and that, that didn't look like a spaceship.

So, the lights go down and the curtains open but not wide, not wide like for Cinemascope, and the movie started and it said, it said Allied Artists and I never heard of Allied Artists, I'd only heard of Warner Bros. and Paramount and Universal and 20th Century Fox and M-G-M, and I think RKO, but Allied Artists I never heard of and maybe, maybe that's why it said Studio Feature Preview and not Major Studio Preview, maybe that was why.

It wasn't in Cinemascope or color, it was, it was in black-and-white, and the title of the movie was *Target Eart*h and it had people I've never heard of in it. Still, still it was a preview and no one but us, us and the rest of the audience were seeing it before it came out, so it was still exciting even though it was Allied Artist and not Cinemascope or color.

It was weird, an empty city, no people, but then four people who are confused, kind of confused like me and fake Rodeo, confused because the city is empty and there's no people in the city because it's empty. Then we found out why, we found out why because there was a big robot in the city and it was, it was, it was dangerous and had a thing that opened and some kind of, some kind of ray beam thing that would pulverize anything it beamed or whatever it did.

The robot wasn't as good as the robot in *The Day the Earth Stood Still*, that was a good robot that wasn't mean or anything, this was a mean robot that pulverized everything and would have pulverized the four people if they weren't saved by, you know, if they weren't saved by the Army. The movie was really short, not long like *The High and the Mighty*, it was really short and I guess it scared some people but not me.

I guess it scared some people because a little boy, maybe he was five or six, this little boy ran up the aisle when the, when the mean robot first appeared, this little boy ran up the aisle and we never saw him again, so it must have been scary but not to me.

That was, that was my, that was my second preview and all the way home mother and father said, they said, they said what a waste of time and money it was, well, father said the thing about money, and how stupid the movie was. I didn't think it was stupid but I liked all movies, but I learned, I learned that from then on, from then on I would only see Major Studio Previews not Studio Feature Previews, just the Major Studio Previews because I figured those were more important than Studio Feature Previews at the Baldwin Theater on La Brea and fake Rodeo.

I think *Target Earth* came out in December, I think, but I, but I never saw it again until, you know, years later on television. It was dopey but I liked it anyway because I'd seen it at a Studio Feature Preview.

Okay, this is, I think this is, this is a good place to stop for now and I'll change cassettes and start again, maybe tomorrow unless there's a Major Studio Preview I have to go see, maybe tomorrow I'll continue because I'm having fun being yakky although I don't know if I'll, if I'll ever, if I'll ever listen to all this yakky whatever it is I'm doing. Shutting the cassette thing off for now.

CASSETTE TWO

Testing. Testing.

Okay, I'm starting another cassette now, I'm starting where I left off, maybe not exactly where I left off but close to where I left off. Anyway, I started high school and it was, you know, it was, it was just like grammar school and junior high school only worse. Some of the mean boys from junior high, some of them were in high school too, the mean boys, and they still madc fun, thcy still made fun of me and threatened me but that's all, that's all it ever was, they never actually killed me like they said they might, you know, it was just threats, but I hated being in school anyway. Same deal, no real friends and didn't like taking classes because I was, because I was impatient and couldn't concentrate on things, to learn things, that's why I didn't really read books or anything because my mind couldn't and can't sit still as you've probably already realized that is if anyone is listening, if anyone is listening to these tapes.

Anyway, you know I never, I never noticed until I started making these records, well, tapes, records of my life I guess you'd call it, until I started making these records of my life, these tapes, I never noticed how much I said the word anyway. Anyway, I'm just, I'm just saying that for the record, that I say anyway a lot. Anyway, in 1955 I was fifteen and I was in high school and I didn't like being there for all the reasons I already said. The only fun for me, the only fun was being in the audio/visual department and, you know, learning to operate a projector and show movies in school, not movies like in theaters, not like that, not normal movies, but school movies, movies they made for schools, those kinds of movies.

Anyway, in 1955 I went to more Major Studio Previews, there was no stopping me and if father or mother didn't want to drive I took buses even though I was fifteen and could get a learner's permit and learn how to drive, father would never let me take the car and so why learn how to drive although I would have learned if he'd let me take the car and eventually I did learn because he, because he finally let me take the car.

Okay, maybe I should admit, maybe I should just admit that, maybe I should admit that while I have a really good memory, when I started going to Major Studio Previews, I started a list of what I saw, you know, a list of what I saw and when and where. I mean, I remember the movies, I never forget a movie ever and even some of the dates and theaters, but I have that on the list and I look at the list while I'm making this record, this cassette tape of this record so that I get it right. I stopped making the lists, I stopped making the lists around 1958 so I may not have so many dates when I get to that part but I'm not to that part so now I'll talk about the

Major Studio Previews I saw in 1955 because that's where we left off when I stopped the first cassette.

So, the first Major Studio Preview I saw, it was on January 7th and I saw the ad in the, I saw the ad in the newspaper, a Major Studio Preview at the Egyptian in Cinemascope and color and I told mother and father we had to go because, because I liked that theater so much and it was Cinemascope and color. As usual, as usual, father complained the whole drive there because it was a long drive, he complained that we were going to the poorhouse and mother and I just laughed because of That's Just Earl, always complaining about money.

Mother was a wonderful, she was a wonderful cook so, so we didn't go out to eat a lot, but since we had to leave as soon as father got home from welding and changed, and changed into his normal clothes, mother and father decided we'd eat out so we wouldn't be late, so we wouldn't be late to see the movie before the Major Studio Preview as father wanted to get his money's worth.

We ate at a drive-in on Sunset and Cahuenga. I don't know why, I don't know why he chose a drive-in but he did because none of us had ever been to a drive-in so why not he said. Scrivner's was the name of the drive-in and we drove in, we drove in and parked and then a pretty girl came and we looked at the menu and ordered and they brought the food to the car and that was interesting, that was weird but I liked eating in the car on a tray, I didn't know you could do that, that you could eat in a car on a tray.

Anyway, I ordered a king size double deck cheeseburger and a malt, a chocolate malt and I'd never had a malt and the double deck cheeseburger and the malt were really good and it was something mother never made so I didn't have to compare it, it was just good and I ate it all and had the entire malt.

Mother had a barbecued beef sandwich, chuck wagon style and father had a chili size, a hamburger with chili all over it but I didn't, I didn't understand the size part. Mother always liked when I cleaned my, when I cleaned my plate and she said look at my growing boy but of course I wasn't growing, I was 5'3" small and going nowhere, so that was funny as long as you weren't 5'3" tall and going nowhere. We all shared a strawberry shortcake although that had nothing to do with me and I don't know why they called it a shortcake. At least I was taller than the shortcake. Anyway, I never forgot that meal at Scrivner's Drive-In, which is why I, which is why I remember it now and don't need it on a list, I remember it exactly and how everything smelled and tasted.

Then we drove to the Egyptian and parked and walked back to the theater. The movie, the movie that was playing there was called *Deep in My Heart* so we saw that before the Major Studio Preview and it was about, it was about someone named Sigmund Romberg who wrote songs and there were so many songs and singing and I just wanted everyone to be quiet because there were so many songs and singing and I thought it would never be over, it would never be over and we'd never see the Major Studio Preview. The best thing about it was the M-G-M sign at the beginning, with the, with the roaring lion, that's why I liked M-G-M movies because they had a roaring lion.

But finally it was over, it was over and we sat and waited and then the lights went out and the curtain opened and opened really wide like for *The High and the Mighty* and that huge Cinemascope screen. It was another M-G-M movie and the lion roared and it was A Cinemascope Production in color and everyone waited to see what the movie was, what we were going to see. The music was, you know, the music was exciting and the first thing we saw was a train from the air like we were in an airplane or something like being in an airplane even though I'd never been in an airplane and the screen was so huge it felt like you were part of the movie. The train came right toward us and as it did the first credit came up and said Spencer Tracy and everyone in the audience seemed really excited, then it, then it said Robert Ryan and they were excited about Robert Ryan too and then we finally, we finally got the title of the movie, *Bad Day at Black Rock*, and I already knew I loved the movie because it was already, it was already so exciting with the music and the train.

And I did love the movie. Spencer Tracy had one good arm and kept his other arm his bad arm in his, in his pocket and everyone was making fun of him and treating him, and treating him like the mean kids treated me and they threatened to kill him and yet with only one arm he beat the living daylights out of the meanest mean man and I loved that, I loved that and I thought maybe if I had one arm I could beat the living daylights out of the mean boys, but I had two arms so that was out of the question.

I was yakky about the movie all the way home and, and in my room I pretended I had one arm and was beating the living daylights out of the mean kids and that's why I loved movies because the good guys beat the living daylights out of the bad guys and that was good, that was satisfying.

But before I tell you about the next Major Studio Preview I want to tell what happened in school because in a way it was, in a way it was like *Bad Day at Black Rock*, only *Bad Day at High School.*

Anyway, anyway, I was walking to my next class, my science class, which I hated, I hated my science class because I didn't, didn't understand anything the teacher was, was talking about. So, I was, I was, I was walking to my science class that I, that I hated and I, I usually kept, I usually kept my head down but my head was up and I saw the worst of the mean boys walking towards me. He didn't have a mean look on his face, though, he was, he was just walking, like walking to his next class, but when he got near me he all of a sudden, all of a sudden out of the blue, all of a sudden out of the blue he just socks me really hard with his fist, on my right cheek near my eye.

I was shocked and dazed because, because it was so all of a sudden out of the blue. I think I almost fell down but I, I didn't, I just kind of, kind of stumbled. Anyway, after he socked me really hard with his fist he just walked on like he'd, like he hadn't socked me really hard with his fist. The next thing I knew, this girl from my, from my science class came up to me, this girl, Louise was her name, she was really tall and had really short hair, like a boy haircut or something, and she looked tough, even in science class she looked tough and she came up to me and said did that moron just hit you?

I was, I was still shocked and dazed but I said it's okay and she said it's not okay, come with me, and I said no, it's okay, really, and she said it's not okay, really, come with me. She started walking towards the mean boy and I guess, I guess I followed behind her as she walked towards the mean boy and suddenly she shouted really loud hey you, moron, you with the crewcut, yeah, you, don't keep walking when I'm talking to you.

This all, this all made me very nervous and I was still shocked and dazed from being socked in the face but there was no stopping this tall girl Louise who looked tough. The mean boy stopped and turned around slowly and I, I thought uh oh, because he looked, he looked really, he looked really mean and angry. But she kept walking up to him, right up to him until she was standing an inch from his face.

She said why'd you hit him, he never did anything to you, and the mean boy sneered and said it's none of your business, and the girl, Louise, said oh yeah, well it is my business when I see you and your friends giving this guy a hard time and then hitting him like that, with no warning, you just hit him like that with no warning.

And she suddenly, suddenly with no warning, socks the mean boy right in the jaw and she said like that, you just hit him like that, with no warning. And the mean boy goes down to the ground, holding his jaw and he's like I was, shocked and dazed. He's on the ground but she just, she just picks him up by his shirt and says listen to me, moron, don't ever bother him again, not you, not your moron friends, understand?

The mean boy shook his head yes and, and there was blood, there was blood coming out of his mouth and dripping on the ground. The girl, Louise, was still holding him by the shirt, she was holding him by the shirt and said if there's a next time you'll be very sorry, you have no idea how sorry you'll be, now get out of my sight.

The mean boy with the blood coming out of his mouth walked, he walked away so fast and Louise said are you okay and I said, I said, I said yeah, I guess, I guess I'm okay. She said c'mon, you'll be late for class and we walked toward the building where science class was. I couldn't believe what she'd, what she'd just done and we must have looked, we must have looked pretty funny walking to class, with me being 5'3" and her being 6'something. All during class, all I could, all I could think of was that I, that I had my own personal Spencer Tracy. And the mean boys never bothered me again.

Anyway, where was I? Oh yeah, the next Major Studio Preview, okay, okay, the next one, well, the next two were, the next two were amazing and I could talk for hours but I won't because I know I talk too much, that I'm a motormouth and yakky, because some things never change.

Anyway, anyway the next one was on May 2nd in Hollywood again so you know what father was saying all the way there about the poorhouse. We ate at home this time, mother's wonderful macaroni and cheese and her, and her wonderful grilled cheese sandwiches the best anywhere, then, then we went to the theater, another theater I'd never been to called the Pantages, another amazing movie palace that was huge and beautiful and that I, that I loved immediately.

Mother and father didn't want to see the movie that was playing, *Strange Lady in Town*, so we got there at 8:00 for the 8:30 preview. The newspaper said a new thing, that this was an IMPORTANT Major Studio Preview in Cinemascope and color, so that, so that was very exciting that it was an IMPORTANT Major Studio Preview in Cinemascope and color.

We found good seats halfway down even though, even though the theater was pretty full. We saw the end of *Strange Lady in Town* and I was glad we didn't see the rest of it because, because it, it didn't, it didn't look that interesting.

Then my favorite part, my favorite part, the house lights went out and the curtain opened really wide and there was the Warner Bros. logo that looked like a shield a knight would carry, so it was a Warner Bros. picture like *The High and the Mighty*. The first thing that happened was a boat on the water, a boat as wide, as wide as Cinemascope, and then a man holding, a man holding binoculars and the whole audience cheered at the man, I guess because they knew who he was and even I knew who he was so I cheered too and mother and father were happy that the man was in the movie. Then the title of the movie came on, *Mister Roberts*, and the audience applauded the title too. Then it said Henry Fonda and James Cagney and, and there was more applause.

Anyway, it was a, it was a, a really great movie. I loved it and mother and father loved it and the audience loved it and there was such loud laughter and even crying and like I said I could, I could go on and on and on for hours about it and I was yakky about it from the time we left the theater until the, until the time I brushed my teeth and got in bed but I couldn't sleep because I was remembering all the scenes, I was remembering all the, all the scenes I loved, which was all of them.

The next Major Studio Preview was on July 11th, that was a Monday and *Mister Roberts* was on a Monday too, so Monday was a good Major Studio Preview day. Anyway, the ad in the paper, the ad in the paper got me really excited because it was another IMPORTANT Major Studio Preview, it was at my wonderful Paramount Theater, and it said in VistaVision and Technicolor and I didn't know what VistaVision meant so that was exciting and I, I, I loved anything in Technicolor because I liked the name Technicolor.

This time, this time we went to see the movie before the preview because we all thought that it sounded like it was really good and fun, *The Seven Little Foys* was the title and Bob Hope was the star and we all, we all loved Bob Hope movies and it was in VistaVision and Technicolor too. The ad said you'd hear it in Perspecta Stereophonic Sound and I, I, I didn't know what that meant but I loved it anyway, just the, just the name of it and it said see it on our NEW CURVILINEAR SCREEN! I didn't know what that meant either but I, but I loved the sound of it.

We got our good seats halfway down and the curtains opened but not wide, not wide and skinny like Cinemascope, but much taller and still wide but not *as* wide and the movie started and first there was the Paramount mountain and then it said VistaVision and below it said Motion Picture High Fidelity and I, I didn't know what that meant but I loved it. I really enjoyed *The Seven Little Foys* because it looked amazing and colorful and, and almost like you were there because, because it was so sharp and, it was so sharp and detailed and like you were there. Mother and father enjoyed it too even though going to all these movies was going to put us in the poorhouse.

Then there was, there was the usual intermission. Mother had already gotten her box of Dots that we would, that mother and I, that we'd share and father got a frozen U-NO bar. I had a frozen U-NO bar once and it was confusing because I didn't know what I was eating. It, it tasted like chocolate covered chalk not that I'd ever eaten chocolate covered chalk but that was what I thought chocolate covered chalk would taste like.

Anyway, the lights went down and they, oh, and they had new curtains, by the way. They had new curtains and one curtain went up and behind the one that went up, behind that there was a second, a second curtain that went sideways like most curtains in movie theaters did. That was, that was really fun the up curtain and the side curtain and made me even more excited to see the IMPORTANT Major Studio Preview in VistaVision and Technicolor on the huge Curvilinear Screen.

The movie started and it was the Paramount mountain again, that was funny because we had a Paramount Picture on the huge Curvilinear Screen and we were in the Paramount Theater. Oh, I, I forgot to mention something because sometimes I forget to mention things because of my mind being a Mexican jumping bean, so I forgot to mention that I loved the music that played over the Paramount mountain and especially the music that played over, that played over the VistaVision logo, so I'm mentioning it.

Then there was a, there was a travel store window with posters showing, posters that showed France and over that it said Cary Grant and Grace Kelly and like had happened with

Mister Roberts and other Major Studio Previews everyone applauded and oohed and aahed when they saw the names.

Mother leaned over and whispered in my, she whispered in my ear Cary Grant is the most handsome man in the entire world, don't tell father I said so. I didn't know Cary Grant was the handsomest man in the world because, because I'd never seen a Cary Grant movie. I didn't, I didn't know who Cary Grant was and I didn't know who Grace Kelly was either. Then came the title of the movie, Alfred Hitchcock's *To Catch a Thief* and there was more oohing and aahing that we were seeing Alfred Hitchcock's *To Catch a Thief* and that was so exciting even though, even though I didn't have, I didn't have any idea who Alfred Hitchcock was.

After the titles, there was a cat walking on a, on a rooftop and then someone was, someone was stealing things and then a woman screamed and said my jewels, my jewels. Anyway, I won't, I won't go on and on about it, but it was, it was the best movie and it was so funny and clever and suspenseful and Grace Kelly was the most beautiful woman I'd ever seen, sorry Veronica Lake, and I wanted to marry her, I wanted to marry her because she was so beautiful even more than Veronica Lake. And mother was right, mother was right that Cary Grant was the handsomest man in the world and together he and Grace Kelly were, they were the most beautiful couple I'd ever seen on the screen or anywhere else.

Later, in August, Alfred Hitchcock's *To Catch a Thief* opened at the Paramount and I saw it three more times, but not there, I saw it at theaters that were, that were, you know, closer to home, closer to our almost house on Rexford.

There were two other Major Studio Previews I saw that year and they were, they were good but not like, not like *Mister Roberts* and *To Catch a Thief* good, just sort of okay good. One was on July 13th at a, at a theater called the Loyola that we'd never been to. It was, it was kind of like a neighborhood theater, very nice but not a, but not a palace. The preview there was in Cinemascope and color, *How to Be Very, Very Popular* was the name of the movie, and Betty Grable was in it and it was, it was kind of funny with girls dressing up as boys and I liked it, it was okay good, but the best thing about it was the song, the title song, that was really fun and I hummed it and it played on the radio all the time and I sang along with it in my yakky voice, just the title, "How to Be Very, Very Popular." I liked the title but I never learned how to be very, very popular or even any kind of popular.

The other Major Studio Preview was at the Village Theater on November 11th in Cinemascope and color and you, you should have, you should have heard the reaction when the movie came on and the entire huge screen was blue and Frank Sinatra was walking and singing a song and then the name of the movie came on and it was called *The Tender Trap*, which is the song he'd been, that he'd been singing while, you know, walking. The movie was cute and a little funny, not good good, but okay good except for the song when the screen was blue, that was, that was really good good.

I saw lots and lots of Major Studio Previews in 1956 and 1957, a lot of them at the, at the, at the Village Theater. The funny thing about seeing Major Studio Previews at the Village Theater was when I'd walk in, when I'd walk in the Village Theater they, they knew me because I was, I was there for so many Major Studio Previews, and they'd wave when I walked in and I liked that they knew me and waved because that made me feel very, very popular.

Some of the Major Studio Previews I saw in 1956 and 1957, were *Bus Stop* with Marilyn Monroe, who I wanted to marry because Grace Kelly went and married, she went and married a prince or something, some prince in some far off place, so I couldn't marry her, but Marilyn Monroe was, she was, she was, well, Marilyn Monroe, so pretty and sexy, that was the word father used, sexy. Mother didn't like that he used that word, she didn't like that at all.

I saw a Major Studio Preview of a picture called *The Girl Can't Help It*, which maybe, which maybe got the most laughs I ever heard in a movie theater and it had someone like Marilyn Monroe but not Marilyn Monroe, kind of a fake Marilyn Monroe, a fake Marilyn Monroe named Jayne Mansfield and she was funny but I didn't want to marry her because she was a fake Marilyn Monroe. In the, in the movie, there were a lot of what they called rock-and-roll songs and it was very colorful and funny. I also saw another Major Studio Preview of a Jayne Mansfield movie called, called *The Wayward Bus*, like a fake *Bus Stop* with a fake Marilyn Monroe, but not a comedy like *The Girl Can't Help It.*

Another, another funny movie I saw at a Major Studio Preview was called *Hollywood or Bust* in VistaVision and Technicolor with Dean Martin and Jerry Lewis. That was a fun Major Studio Preview. Oh, I forgot to say but I'll say it now while I'm thinking about it otherwise I, I might forget to say it so I'll say it now, sometime around then I began, I began to, to take notice of other credits, like, like, like writers and composers and especially directors and I noticed that *Hollywood or Bust* was directed by the same director who directed *The Girl Can't Help It*, Frank Tashlin. I wanted to, I wanted to see all his movies because he made really funny movies and I, and I liked really funny movies where everyone laughed. I bet that maybe I was the only sixteen-year-old who knew that Frank Tashlin made, made really funny movies.

I saw a Major Studio Preview of a, of a suspenseful and good robbery picture that was, that was like nothing I'd ever seen before. It was called *The Killing*, and it kept me on the, on the edge of my seat, not really on the edge of my seat, that's just a saying, but it was really suspenseful and kept me on the edge of my seat and it was in plain old black-and-white, not color or Technicolor, but it suited the movie and I, I never minded black-and-white, I even liked Cinemascope movies in black-and-white.

The year I graduated high school, that was a good year because it meant that I didn't have to go to high school anymore, and it was a good year for seeing Major Studio Previews. That was, that was 1957 and that year, the year I graduated high school, I saw lots of Major Studio Previews and I was, I was, I was old enough to know that some movies, even though I loved movies, not all movies were great or even good good or okay good, some movies were just, well, you know, just plain stinkers, not that I ever, not that I ever didn't sit through even the stinkers.

Anyway, the Major Studio Previews I saw that year were *Bernardine* with Pat Boone who I liked when he sang songs, which he did in *Bernardine*, which was an okay good movie, *Desk Set* with Spencer Tracy with both arms and Katharine Hepburn, those two were at the Village Theater, *The Spirit of St. Louis*, I loved that one because I, I loved James Stewart movies and he was, he was practically the whole movie, just him and his airplane and a fly who kept him company, *Will Success Spoil Rock Hunter?* with fake Marilyn Monroe Jayne Mansfield and Tony Randall, another Major Studio Preview that got some of the, some of the biggest laughs I ever heard and was directed by, you know, by Frank Tashlin.

I missed a lot of Major Studio Previews because I was, you know, I was graduating high school and mother and father were worried that if, that if I, if I didn't do all my schoolwork I wouldn't graduate, so they said no Major Studio Previews until you graduate, and I did graduate with mostly C grades and one D, and mother and father came to graduation and I, I threw my cap in the air and that was the end of school and that was reason enough, that was reason enough to throw your graduation cap in the air.

Oh, and caps, let me talk about that because it's important I talk about caps. In my final semester of high school, I bought my, I bought my first baseball cap and I'll, I'll tell you why I bought my first baseball cap.

I, I bought it because I was starting to lose, you know, starting to lose my hair in the front of my head. Father was almost completely bald and I guess, I guess I inherited his genes or head or something because my hair began disappearing when I was, when I was sixteen. It was very confusing to, to lose your hair at sixteen and it got worse when I turned seventeen and so, and so mother took me to a sporting goods store and we bought a, we bought a baseball cap for me to wear and then, well, you know how it goes with That's Just Harvey, I fixated on the baseball cap and had to, had to wear it everywhere, everywhere all the time, even at school even though I got sent to the principal's office because wearing caps or hats was against the rules, but mother wrote a long note and then they, they let me do it because mother wrote a long note. So, I was never without my baseball cap, not even in the house, not even when I brushed my teeth, only when I went to bed because, because it's hard to sleep with a, with a, you know, with a baseball cap on your head.

Oh, my, my baseball cap was an official Hollywood Stars baseball team baseball cap with an H on the front of it. I never saw the Hollywood Stars baseball team play, they, they played at Gilmore Field, and as luck would have it, as luck would have it, the team stopped playing at the, at the end of the 1957 season and they, they tore Gilmore Field down, they tore it down and built CBS, you know, CBS Studios on that entire corner, so I never saw the Hollywood Stars play even though I had a Hollywood Stars baseball cap with an H on it, H for Hollywood.

I loved that Hollywood Stars baseball cap with the H on it, I loved it and, and I still love it and wear it and I'll wear it until it, until it falls apart. Anyway, let's not talk about that now because there are, there are other things to talk about, like the, like the day I got a draft notice in the mail when I turned eighteen, you know, to report to the draft office or whatever it was, for a, for a, you know, for a physical and mental examination.

I told mother and father I did not want to go to a, to a draft office for a physical and mental examination and I did not want to be in the Army or anything else because it, it made me nervous and I, I knew everyone would make fun of me and give me a, you know, give me a hard time like I had in school.

But they told me I had to go, that it was, that it was, that it was illegal not to go and I could be thrown in jail if I, if I didn't report to the draft office place.

So, I reported to the draft office place on the day and time the notice said I had to come. It was early in the morning and I, I was, I was really nervous, I was really nervous and they kept telling me to take off my Hollywood Stars baseball cap and I wouldn't, I wouldn't take off my Hollywood Stars baseball cap and that made them angry but I still wouldn't take it off.

There were a lot of us there and we all had to take a test, a mental test, a mental test with lots of questions. I didn't like the questions and I was too impatient to even read them, so I, so I just put any answers that came into my head, even though they had, even though they had nothing to do with the questions that I hadn't even read. I'm sure they didn't like my answers because they had nothing to do with the questions.

Then they said take off your clothes for the physical examination, and they told me again to take off my Hollywood Stars baseball cap and I, I told them again I, I told them I don't take off my baseball cap or clothes in front of other people and that was the truth, not even in gym class, I would not even do that in gym class and mother had to send a note to gym class saying I would not do that and I never did that. They yelled at me to take off my baseball cap and clothes and I said I don't do that and that they could, you know, that I could bring a note from mother but that I don't do that. They sent me to the psychiatrist.

The psychiatrist was in a little room, a little green room, all the walls were green. The psychiatrist asked a lot of questions like why wouldn't I take off my baseball cap or clothes and I just sat there and, and told him why and he listened to the way I answered and then asked me if I was retarded and I said no I'm not retarded, I just have a condition and the doctors don't have a name for it so we call it That's Just Harvey. He wrote down everything I was, you know, everything I was saying on a pad.

All I wanted, all I wanted was to get out of there, but he kept, he kept asking me questions I didn't like. He asked me if I was, if I was afraid to go in the Army, to be a man, and I told him I didn't like guns or war movies and if they put a gun in my hand that I'd probably shoot someone in the face, you know, accidentally, and that I didn't care about being a man.

Finally, he told me I could, he told me I could leave and that I'd get a letter telling me what was what. I thanked him for being a psychiatrist in a small room with green walls, and I got out of there so fast, even faster than Superman and a speeding bullet.

Four weeks later, we got a, we got a letter saying the Army didn't want me, that I was 4F due to being a paranoid schizophrenic with homosexual tendencies. That's what it said, that's what the paper said, and they didn't want me because they were probably scared that I'd shoot someone in the face and that I didn't care about the Army or being a man. I didn't know what a paranoid schizophrenic was and I didn't know what homosexual tendencies were, but mother assured me I wasn't a paranoid schizophrenic and that as far as she could tell, I didn't have homosexual tendencies because homosexual tendencies meant you liked other men and that was silly because I wanted to marry Veronica Lake, Grace Kelly, and Marilyn Monroe and I didn't want to marry Cary Grant, James Stewart or Henry Fonda.

Anyway, as mother said, I dodged a bullet and I...

CASSETTE THREE

Testing, testing.

Sorry, the tape, the tape ended and then I had some Campbell's chicken noodle soup, a Swiss cheese sandwich with mustard on Weber's Bread, my favorite, my favorite sandwich, and I had my usual cottage cheese with paprika sprinkled on it, which I always have with my, with my Swiss cheese sandwich on Weber's Bread.

Did I ever mention that I'm recording this in 1968, that I bought this machine, this cassette thing in 1968? I think I did but just in case I didn't, now I, now I am, just so you know what year it is when I'm making this record on these cassette tapes, this record of my past and all the Major Studio Previews. Not that many people have cassette recorder machines. They're a great invention and hopefully, hopefully they'll become popular because they're a great invention especially for people like me, who want to make a record of things on a cassette tape.

Anyway, where was I? I made a note here where I stopped. Oh yeah, here it is. I dodged a bullet and so did the Army because now I wouldn't shoot anyone in the face accidentally.

Mother thought I should start thinking about college and because of my bad, because of my bad grades I could go to a junior college like Santa Monica College or Los Angeles City College, but I didn't want to start thinking about that because I, I didn't want to go, I didn't want to go to any more schools because nothing was going to change and people would make fun of me and I'd be miserable.

So, mother said that father said that I'd have to get a job to make ends meet and I didn't mind thinking about getting a job, even though, even though I had, I had no idea where or even how to get a job. Mother thought about it and said you like music, you could apply for a job at a music store like Wallichs Music City. That might be something you like.

Remember that TV program *Father Knows Best*? Not in our house, in our house Mother Knows Best and she was right, a job in a music store would be right up my alley, as she put it. So, she drove me to Wallichs Music City and I applied for a job. I had to, I had to fill out, to fill out an application and then a nice man named Walter, he had a nametag that said Walter that's how I knew his name was Walter, interviewed me, asking me all kinds of, all kinds of questions, one after another, but it, but it wasn't like the draft office questions, these were okay questions and I answered every question he asked.

Nametag Walter said, he said I, I seemed like a good candidate for being an employee—I liked that word employee—at Wallichs Music City and that I'd start in the back, in the stock room, filing records, LPs and 45s and making store copies that customers could play in the, in the listening booths. I only had one question, could I wear my Hollywood Stars baseball cap in the, in the stock room and Nametag Walter laughed and said that would be, that would be fine. He said I could start in a week, on the following Monday and to be there at 9:00 sharp and I, I, I told him thank you and I'd be there at 9:00 sharp and he said rain or shine and I laughed and said rain or shine.

I told mother when we got in the car and she was thrilled that I had a job at Wallichs Music City and thrilled that Nametag Walter had been so, so nice and he said to be there at 9:00 the following Monday, rain or shine. Mother said he seems to have taken a shine to you, and you get to wear your baseball cap. I told her I'd be, I'd be making minimum wage, one dollar an hour and working forty hours a week. I was so happy I thought I would, I thought I would burst.

Mother stopped at the Farmers Market and we went to the pizza place she liked, Patsy D'Amore's, where we'd gone a few times when I was young. That was her favorite, Patsy D'Amore's, and we both got two slices of cheese pizza and sat at a little table in the, in the sunshine and ate them, you know, to, to celebrate my getting a job at Wallichs Music City. It was, it was the best day.

I had to take driving lessons immediately and that made me nervous but father said they, that they weren't going to the poorhouse having to drive me and pick me up every day and it was, it was too hard to, too hard to get there by bus. So, I went to A-1 Driving School for five days and learned how to drive. And after all that, after all that worrying about it, I, I, I took to it pretty quickly and I took my driving test and they said I passed with flying colors.

It was, it was decided that mother would drive me and pick me up for the first week at, at Wallichs Music City and that father would buy me a cheap used car that wouldn't put us in the poorhouse, but that I, that I would have to, you know, I would have to pay for gas myself out of my paycheck.

Anyway, that's what happened. I loved my job at Wallichs Music City, I was never late, rain or shine, I learned how to file records, how to make store copies for, for the listening booths, and I learned where everything in the store was. Mother drove me and picked me up that first week and then, and then father presented me with a cheap used car, a 1953 chocolate brown two-door Plymouth Cranbrook Belvedere with low mileage and only a few, only a few minor dents, a few minor dents here and there.

I loved my new old chocolate brown two-door Plymouth Cranbrook Belvedere so much, I loved it so much and it was, it was easy to, easy to drive, because once I learned how to shift gears I could, I could, you know, I could do it easily because once I, once I learn something, or do something then That's Just Harvey sets in and that's, and that's that.

Five days a week I drove myself to Wallichs Music City and worked in the back room and Nametag Walter always told me I was doing a fine job, I was, I was a good employee and he was, he was proud of me. I got to hear lots of music, all the new songs and albums too, and that was, and that was, as mother put it, the icing on the cake.

But the best part was, the best part was that I could now drive myself wherever I wanted as long as I paid for gas and I paid for gas so I could go to any Major Studio Preview I wanted to, as I got off work at five and had weekends off, except, except when sometimes Nametag Walter would ask me to work, to work on a Saturday, which was fine with me.

Anyway, in 1958 and 1959, I saw so many wonderful Major Studio Previews including a few IMPORTANT Major Studio Previews. Some were great, some were what I called good good, some were what I called okay good, and some were, some were just plain bad with no good and those were stinkers but I didn't care, I liked seeing all of them even the stinkers.

But, but, but I won't talk about the stinkers, I'll just talk about, I'll just talk about the ones that I, the ones that I really liked, like *Bell, Book and Candle* with my favorite, James Stewart and a lady I hadn't seen before, Kim Novak who was so pretty I wanted to marry her, *The Fly* in Cinemascope and color, scary and weird with a man with a big fly head and a little fly with a big man head and that was, that was disturbing, *Some Came Running*, I loved it with Frank Sinatra and Dean Martin without Jerry Lewis and a new girl who was very good named Shirley MacLaine, I liked her but didn't want to marry her, Alfred Hitchcock's *Vertigo*, James Stewart and Kim Novak again and I really wanted, I *really* wanted to marry Kim Novak after *Vertigo* because there were two of her and the movie was so good, one of the best movies I'd seen, so mysterious and beautiful in VistaVision and Technicolor and I wanted to go and live in San Francisco in James Stewart's apartment with the red door and I, I wanted to have a, I wanted to have a big steak at Ernie's, and I saw it five times once it came out. Another one was *Auntie Mame*, that one was really funny and loud and, and the audience laughed loud and I laughed loud even though I'd never, I'd never seen any of the actors before and I'd never heard such loud actors before. Those were, those were all in 1958 and a lot of them were at the Village Theater where everyone waved to me and seemed happy to, happy to, you know, happy to see me.

Some of the good ones in 1959 were *Anatomy of a Murder* in black-and-white with James Stewart and a beautiful girl named Lee Remick and that was, that was just about the most adult picture I'd ever seen, with words I didn't understand like rape and Mrs. Manion's panties and irresistible impulse, and it was, it was very long but I loved every second of it and saw it two more times after it came out and I still loved it. Another black-and-white Major Studio Preview I saw was called *Some Like It Hot* and I thought I'd heard big laughs in other movies, but this one, this one had laughs so loud it practically, it practically shook the theater, one big laugh after another and sometimes I was laughing so hard tears were coming out of my eyes and I could barely catch my breath and I could barely catch my breath every time Marilyn Monroe was on the screen and she was so beautiful that I wanted to leap into the screen and marry her right there. That was, that was maybe the best preview I'd ever seen and the audience coming out of the theater was buzzing like a, like a, like a beehive about how great it was.

Also, *A Hole in the Head* with Frank Sinatra and I bought the 45 of the song from it, "High Hopes" because it was, because it was so catchy and employees got a nice discount if we, if we bought something. Another Major Studio Preview was *Journey to the Center of the Earth* and I loved it except when the mean villain ate Gertrude the goose, that was disturbing. And *Rio Bravo*, a, a, fun western with John Wayne and Dean Martin and Ricky Nelson from *Ozzie and Harriet* on TV, that was a really good western. At Christmas time I saw a, I saw a Jerry Lewis movie called *Visit to a Small Planet* at the Village Theater and that was interesting because, because the ad in the paper said Major Studio Preview and then it had, it had a, a funny drawing of Jerry Lewis, so we knew it was going to be a Jerry Lewis movie and I liked Jerry Lewis, he was funny but that was the first time I'd ever seen a Major Studio Preview tell who the star was.

Then I saw a preview called *Come Dance With Me*, that one was not a Major Studio Preview because it was a foreign film and it said Foreign Film Preview Tonite even though everyone was speaking English in the foreign film, though their mouths weren't really matching the words that were coming out of them, which, which was confusing and disturbing at the same time, but the lead girl was so sexy and beautiful, Brigitte Bardot was her name and I wanted to marry her, and mother, who went with me, thought it was very racy and wanted to leave but I didn't want to leave because whatever racy was was okay by me.

Another Major Studio Preview was *A Summer Place*, a Warner Bros. picture and I also bought the 45 of the theme, Percy Faith's version, which was our number one selling 45 at Wallichs Music City. The movie was okay good but the theme was catchy and that's what I, that's what I really liked. Then I saw a Major Studio Preview called *Blue Denim*, in Cinemascope and black-and-white, another adult movie where a teenage girl got pregnant and they tried to get her an abortion. I'd, I'd never heard the word pregnant or abortion before in a movie, so it was like *Anatomy of a Murder*, like that kind of adult movie and I liked adult movies like that.

I asked mother about those things, about rape and Mrs. Manion's panties and pregnant and abortion and irresistible impulse, but she told me she, she told me she couldn't discuss such words and subjects with me, with her own son even if her own son was now nineteen and should have, should have known about all those things. I went to the library over on Robertson and did some, some research so now I knew about those things.

Anyway, that takes us, that takes us to 1960 and that's kind of when everything changed in a lot of ways. From 1960 on, those were the start of what I call, of what I call the glory years for me and previews, where my, my fixation with previews really became, well, really became, well, really became my life, what I lived for, all I cared about and it was the time, those years, it was the time when I realized there were others like me, well, maybe not like me exactly, maybe they didn't have my That's Just Harvey condition, but others who went to Major Studio Previews the way I did, others who, who shared my, my fixation, others, others who lived only for previews. That was a big surprise and I got to, I mean we became sort of our own, our own little group of, of preview nuts, that was our name for ourselves, preview nuts but there I go again jumping ahead but there's nothing I can do about it because my mind, my mind just does whatever it wants to, like a Mexican jumping bean and it's just, it's just the way it is when your mind does what it wants to and you're a yakky motormouth.

Oh, wait, I have to go now, there's a Major Studio Preview in Westwood at the, at the Plaza Theater and I, I don't, I don't want to be, I don't want to be late. I'll do more when I, when I come home.

Back from the preview, a movie called *Fade In* and all I'll say is it was a stinker, it was, it was, well, people walked out, like most of the audience walked out but not me because I don't walk out of movies because I think you should always stay to the end even if they're stinkers like *Fade In*. I did see a few of my fellow preview nuts there, so that was nice but I haven't talked about my fellow preview nuts yet, and I saw the guy from Paramount Studios who came up to me and asked what I thought and I told him, and they always, they always knew I'd tell them, that I'd tell them the truth and I told him the truth that I thought it was, I thought it was a stinker. He laughed and said don't tell anyone, but just between you and me and the projection booth, we're going to shelve it, especially after tonight.

Oh, wait, you don't know why someone, someone from, from Paramount Studios asked me what I thought because,

because I haven't talked about any of that yet so let's go back to where we were, back to 1960, where we were before I saw the stinker Major Studio Preview of *Fade In*, which the guy from Paramount Studios told me wouldn't be, wouldn't be released because they were shelving it.

Anyway, I turned twenty in 1960. Mother said she, that she couldn't believe it that her little boy was all grown up and twenty and that she now, that she now felt so old, but I told her, I told her she was still pretty and not old at all.

Anyway, I was twenty and working at, you know, I was working at Wallichs Music City and making forty dollars a week, and I had my 1953 chocolate brown Plymouth Cranbrook Belvedere that got me where I needed to go, although, although gas prices had gone up to thirty-six cents for ethyl and father complained about it nightly but I never complained because, I never complained because what was the use of complaining, I mean, you had to have gas in the car and they could charge whatever they, they could charge whatever they wanted and besides, I tried never to complain about anything because what was the use?

Anyway, like I said, 1960 was the start of, the start of what I call the glory years when some interesting things happened, and the first, the first interesting thing that happened in 1960 was when I saw a Major Studio Preview of a movie called *The Bellboy*, at the Village. It was another Jerry Lewis picture but this time, at this preview, at this preview after it was over and we all went outside in front of the theater, I was standing there, I was standing there and happened to look over to my left and there was, I couldn't believe it, there was Jerry Lewis himself, in person, right there outside the theater, talking to a few people.

I tried to get closer but everyone, everyone was gawking at him, but I, I, I managed to finally get near Jerry Lewis and he, he looked over at me and saw my Hollywood Stars baseball cap and that I was 5'3" and I, I guess, I guess he thought that was funny because he smiled at me and I said Mr. Lewis, Mr. Lewis, I loved the movie and I've seen a lot of Major Studio Previews and this was one of, this was one of the funniest and I think it will be a big hit.

He looked at me, I guess you'd call it quizzically and who could blame him when someone in a Hollywood Stars baseball cap suddenly just said something out of the blue. But then he smiled again and said thanks, from your mouth to God's ears. Then he asked what's your name?

I said Harvey, my name is Harvey and I go to Major Studio Previews, that's what I do, I go to Major Studio Previews. He smiled again and said well, Preview Harvey, I hope you'll be at all my previews. He turned to his friends or whoever they were and said this is Preview Harvey, he goes to lots of previews and he loved the movie and thinks it will be a big hit. Everyone looked over at me and smiled and, and said hello. Finally, Jerry Lewis said to me you know, Preview Harvey, this is the first movie I've directed, so I just want you to know that you liking it means a lot.

I stood there and couldn't believe, I couldn't believe Jerry Lewis talked to me and I couldn't believe I talked to him, just said things out of the blue. As I walked back to my car, for the first time I, I felt like I was six feet tall even though I was, well, you know, 5'3". But I couldn't stop thinking about what he'd called me, Preview Harvey, I couldn't stop thinking about it and I thought about it all the way driving home, I was, you know, I was fixated on it. Preview Harvey, that's what Jerry Lewis called me. Preview Harvey.

When I got home, I told mother all about it and how Jerry Lewis was at the Major Studio Preview and that, and that he'd talked to me and that he called me Preview Harvey. Mother thought that was a perfect name for me, Preview Harvey, and I knew right then, I knew right then that that was going to be my name when I went to previews, Preview Harvey. And it wasn't just me who knew my name was Preview Harvey because apparently Jerry Lewis had told everyone at Paramount Studios about me and the next time I was at a preview of a Paramount movie, *The Rat Race* with Tony Curtis and Debbie Reynolds, after the movie in the lobby of the Wiltern Theater, a man came up to me and said, you're Preview Harvey, aren't you and I, I said, I said yes, how did you know I'm Preview Harvey and he said he'd heard about me and he worked at Paramount Studios and what did I think of *The Rat Race* and I told him I thought it was, I thought it was very good and that I especially liked the music. He said he was very pleased to hear it and, and looked forward to seeing me, to seeing me at more previews.

But then another interesting thing happened. I was at the Village seeing a Major Studio Preview in Cinemascope and color and the Major Studio Preview was a movie called *High Time*, with Bing Crosby although I didn't care about Bing Crosby, not when there was, not when there was an adorable girl in the picture with the funny name of Tuesday Weld and of course I wanted to marry her because she was adorable. The movie got lots of big laughs and I loved it, mostly because of Tuesday Weld, whose last name, whose last name was what father did for a living, that was funny.

After the movie, I was, I was standing outside the theater, hoping that Tuesday Weld might be there in person, like Jerry Lewis had been there in person, but I didn't see her. But one of the ushers who knew me, one of the ushers who knew me came up to me and pointed to a man and he said that was the, that the man he was pointing to was the director of the movie, Blake Edwards. I thought about whether I should, whether I should tell him I liked his movie, but he was, he was talking to people and I, I, didn't want to interrupt but I just detoured over towards him and pretended, I pretended I'd just walked out of the theater even though I'd already walked out of the theater and as I was just about to walk past him I just said excuse me Mr. Edwards, I see a lot of Major Studio Previews and I just wanted to say that I loved your movie *High Time*. He looked up at me, well, down at me really, and said thanks kid, that's very nice of you to say and glad you liked it and I said I loved it and it was really funny and he said thank you and I'm glad you liked it and then I just walked on and went to my car.

When I got home, I told mother I'd met a movie director named Blake Edwards and she was, she was very impressed that I'd met a movie director, even though she'd never heard of him.

I was, I was going to as many Major Studio Previews as I could. I'd work all day and then I'd, I'd drive to whatever theater and see a Major Studio Preview. Some of the others I saw in 1960 were *The Crowded Sky*, which was kind of a, kind of a version of *The High and the Mighty* but not nearly as good, *Midnight Lace* with Doris Day being scared because someone was trying to, you know, trying to torment her and kill her or something, with a surprise ending, *Strangers When We Meet*, that one I liked because Kim Novak was in it. With mother and father, I saw *The Subterraneans*, and they didn't like it at all because it was about beatniks and they thought beatniks were nasty and the end of civilized society, but I liked it because, I liked it because Leslie Caron was in it and I'd seen other movies with her like *Gigi* and *Daddy Long Legs* and she was so cute and perky but in this picture she was a beatnik.

Then there was *Village of the Damned* and I loved *Village of the Damned* because it had creepy blonde children with glowing eyes in black-and-white and the creepy blonde children's eyes would glow and make people do bad things, like shoot themselves in the face with a shotgun. That was one of my favorites and when it, when it came out, I saw it eight more times.

Then came 1961, and that was a, that was a very good year for Major Studio Previews and even more interesting things happened that year. So, let me tell you about the first interesting thing that happened before I tell you about the Major Studio Previews and the other interesting things that happened. The first interesting thing that happened was in June of 1961 at a, at a Major Studio Preview of a picture called *Voyage to the Bottom of the Sea* at the Village. Anyway, I liked the movie a lot because it had a nuclear submarine and I'd never seen a nuclear submarine before and so I liked the movie and I liked Peter Lorre, because he had a funny voice and he was, he was short like me.

After the movie, I walked out of the theater to see if anyone from the movie was there, but I didn't see anyone from the movie. Just as I was about to leave, a fellow came up to me and said that he'd been seeing me at Major Studio Previews for the past couple of years and that he went to Major Studio Previews too, he was sixteen and that was his life, all he cared about, going to Major Studio Previews. I didn't know there was anyone else like me, that was, that lived for Major Studio Previews. I told him maybe we were two of a kind and that I'd been fixated on going to Major Studio Previews since I was fourteen, and he told me he was fixated too, and that there wasn't anything better than going to Major Studio Previews. Then I, I told him how Jerry Lewis had been at the preview of *The Bellboy* and that I'd been yakky and told him how much I liked his movie and that he'd named me Preview Harvey right where we were standing, right near the box-office of the, of the Village Theater.

The fellow said his name was Nate Fahr. Now, like I've already mentioned a million zillion times, I have a condition called That's Just Harvey. I'll probably mention it a million zillion more times. Anyway, Nate Fahr had a condition too, and I noticed it right away because you, because you couldn't really miss it, his condition.

What his condition was, well, he had this kind of shudder thing, this uncontrollable shudder thing. I don't know if, if shudder is the right word, jerk, maybe jerk is the right word, his body jerks, he can't control it, it just happens, this sudden jerky thing his body does happens, like a spasm, maybe that's a better word, spasm, anyway whatever it is happens and then it's over until it happens again which is a lot.

It was a little, it was a little unnerving at first, the jerking or spasm or whatever it was. Even more unnerving was that sometimes, well, sometimes words would just blurt out of him and sometimes they were not nice words that I won't repeat on this cassette. The not nice words would just, would just blurt out of him and he had no control over that either. It just happened and people would look at him funny because they didn't know he had a condition that causes him to jerk or spasm and have things just blurt out of his mouth. They just thought he was weird, just like people thought I was weird, and he told me they made fun of him in school and I told him that happened to me too, and he told me when he was a, when he was a kid the doctors were, the doctors were, were baffled by his condition and that it didn't really have a name just like mine didn't have a real name, just the name mother had come up with, That's Just Harvey. I told him that made us, made us even more two of a kind.

Anyway, I won't say that we became friends because we didn't, but we were preview nuts together from then on and would see each other at Major Studio Previews and talk about the movies we'd seen or maybe we'd gone to different Major Studio Previews and we'd talk about that and he'd tell me about his movie and I'd, I'd tell him about my movie and it was, it was, you know, it was nice to have someone to talk to.

We never sat together at Major Studio Previews though. He had the seat he liked and I had the seat I liked and they were in, they were in different parts of the theater, but before the preview and after the preview we'd talk, sometimes in the, in the lobby and sometimes in the theater. And then we found some other preview nuts but that happened, that happened later and I'm talking about now, not now now but 1961 now.

Anyway, that's how that all began so now you know about that interesting thing. Nate and I, Nate and I saw each other quite a bit at Major Studio Previews from then on. That was in, that was in June, like I said. But before that, another interesting thing happened and that interesting thing was that I got a big surprise at work from Nametag Walter, my, my boss. Here's what, here's what that interesting thing was.

It was a, it was a Friday and I'd worked all week so I had Saturday and Sunday off and I was, I was wrapping things up. I'd done, I'd done all my usual stuff, filing, making listening copies, going in the listening booths and getting the albums that people left in there and putting them, putting them back where they belonged, you know, all my usual stuff that I did every day.

Nametag Walter came up to me with a serious face and said he needed to talk to me privately and I got, I got very nervous, I got very nervous thinking maybe, maybe I did something wrong or didn't do something I should have done. Anyway, he took me into a small office and closed the door and told me to have a, to have a seat, that this was, this was going to be an important conversation and that made me, that made me even more nervous than the nervous I already was.

He sat down across from me and said we've thought about this very carefully and this is not something we do lightly and oh boy, oh boy was I getting more, getting more nervous. He said let me preface this by saying that you have been an excellent employee, you've always been on time, you've never asked to leave early, and everyone, including me, is so happy to have you with us and you're such an asset to the store. So, why did I feel like my head was in a, was in a, you know, one of those, those things that cuts your head off?

Then Nametag Walter said with a serious voice we don't do these things lightly, then he paused, then he said but we're giving you a twenty-five-cent raise in salary and we hope you'll be with us for a long time. I, I, I couldn't believe it, a twenty-five-cent raise, and out of the blue, completely out of the blue. Then he said I got them to prorate it as of last week, so your raise will be reflected on this week's paycheck. Congratulations and you should feel very good about it because frankly it doesn't happen here all that often.

But that wasn't all because he continued talking and said there's one more thing you should know that just happened. Minimum wage has gone up to $1.15, so, with your raise, you'll now be making $1.40 an hour. How's that?

I let out a big breath, a, a sigh of relief, as mother would say, like when she had heartburn and took Pepto Bismol and felt better and didn't want to eat the head of a chicken she'd let out a big sigh of relief, and I said I thought you were going to fire me because you had such a, such a serious face and voice. Nametag Walter laughed and said I know, I was just having some fun acting serious. Now, don't spend it all in one place, especially at Wallichs Music City.

And that was that and he said I could, he said I could leave early and go celebrate and I don't think anyone on earth had a more, a more wonderful boss than Nametag Walter. I drove right home, trying not to, trying not to speed and when I walked in the door, mother looked at me and said well, you look like the cat who got the cream, what's going on? I said you're looking at an employee of Wallichs Music City who just got a raise out of the blue, that's what's going on. She said a raise, that's wonderful, that's just wonderful. I said twenty-five cents, that was, that was my raise. She said twenty-five cents, that is incredible because nobody these days wants to pay a penny over minimum wage. I'm so proud of you I could cry, but she didn't cry. I said that's the, that's the other, the other thing. She said what other thing? I said minimum wage. It's gone up to a dollar-fifteen so I'll, so with the, with the raise, I'll be making a dollar-forty an hour. She said you're a regular Rockefeller and she said good work and hard work always pays dividends. Let's tell father and go out and celebrate.

I said we'd have to do it right away, celebrate, because, because I had a Major Studio Preview to go to at the Beverly Theater. She said you can miss one preview for a celebration, and there'll be plenty of previews over the weekend. I thought about it for a minute and said okay I'll miss the Major Studio Preview but it will, it will probably be the best movie ever made and she said it could also be the worst movie ever made and I said that if I didn't go it's all I'd, it's all I'd think about at dinner, so she said fine we'll all go to the preview. Then she told father about the raise and minimum wage going up and he said good for you and then we all went to dinner at 6:00 at, at Nate 'n Al's in real Beverly Hills, just up the street from the Beverly Theater, where the Major Studio Preview was.

Nate 'n Al's was a Jewish delicatessen even though we were currently atheists. I'd never been to a Jewish delicatessen so I, so I had no idea what to order, what kind of food to eat. They had, they had so many things on the menu to choose from, I couldn't, I couldn't decide and asked the waitress, who looked like a mummy, what she thought an atheist might like in a Jewish deli. She recommended the matzoh ball soup and a corned beef sandwich on rye with mustard. I didn't know what any of that meant, so I said okay. Mother ordered a brisket of beef sandwich and coleslaw, and father ordered a club sandwich, which he, which he thought was a bargain because, because you got three pieces of bread.

The matzoh ball soup was, it was, it was kind of like Campbell's chicken noodle soup but with big chunks of chicken with a big ball floating in it and it was very tasty and so was the big ball, the big matzoh ball laying there in the soup. Mother looked at it and said look at the size of that ball and father laughed and mother looked at him and said what's so funny, but he, but he didn't say what was so funny but kept laughing. Since he never really laughed all that much, we all joined in laughing, even though we, even though we didn't know what was funny.

I also enjoyed the corned beef sandwich on rye bread with mustard. I'd, I'd never tasted anything quite like corned beef. Anyway, it was a very good meal and mother said maybe we should be Jews. After we finished and father paid the check after, you know, after complaining how expensive it was, we all just walked down to the Beverly Theater and got there just in time for the, for the Major Studio Preview.

We were, we were a little further back than usual because we were late, but the, but the seats were fine and we could see the screen and the person, the person in front of me wasn't too tall, which was sometimes a problem, given my, given my height or lack of it. Anyway, the, the Major Studio Preview was called *Fanny* and that made father laugh too and mother hit him hard on the arm and told him he wasn't in kindergarten. Leslie Caron, the beatnik from, from *The Subterraneans*, wasn't a beatnik in *Fanny*, she was Fanny in *Fanny* and so cute

I wanted to marry her. I enjoyed it and the Technicolor color was beautiful, better than real-life color. I also loved the music and when the movie finally opened, we got the soundtrack LP in at Wallichs Music City and I, I bought it thanks to my twenty-five-cent raise and the new minimum wage.

Before meeting my, my fellow preview nut, Nate, I'd seen some great Major Studio Previews and a few that were just okay good. My favorites were a movie called *The Great Impostor* with Tony Curtis as a great impostor, who pretended he was other people and everyone believed him and he was a doctor, a prison warden, a monk, all kinds of people he wasn't. It was funny and had drama and was in black-and-white and it was, it was excellent and so was *The Last Time I Saw Archie*, both those Major Studio Previews were at the Picwood, where I saw quite a few Major Studio Previews, and *The Last Time I Saw Archie* was in black-and-white too and it was fun and had a song I liked called "At Last."

Then there was the weirdest, the weirdest western I'd ever seen called *One-Eyed Jacks* and it was, it was really long and just plain weird and Marlon Brando was weird and I couldn't understand a lot of what he was saying, although, although I did understand when he called someone a tub of guts, I thought, I thought that was a good thing to, to call someone if you, if you didn't like them. That one I saw at the Paramount Theater in VistaVision and Technicolor and I thought, I thought it was beautiful to watch, good scenery, and the music was good too, but I just, I just didn't know what to make of the whole thing.

That same man from Paramount Studios was at that preview and he didn't seem too happy with the audience reaction. He'd seen me in the lobby afterwards and he came right up to me and said, Preview Harvey, I'm afraid to ask what you thought of it but go ahead and tell me. I told him I thought it was, I thought it was beautiful to watch and I liked the scenery and music, but that the story was, the story was a little confusing and weird, at least to me it was, and I couldn't understand too much of Marlon Brando except for, except for tub of guts. He said just between you and me and the projection booth—that was his, that was his regular line to me, just between you and me and the projection booth—and he said I think we've got a stiff on our hands and I didn't know what stiff meant but he said a stiff, like a dead body. He told me he thought I had good movie sense and I, I didn't know that I had good movie sense, so that was good to know.

A few other Major Studio Previews I liked were *Wild in the Country* with Elvis Presley but I didn't care about that, I liked it because, I liked it because Tuesday Weld was in it, and she was, she was still adorable and I wanted to meet Tuesday Weld but she wasn't at the preview and neither was Elvis Presley. *The Naked Edge* with Gary Cooper and Deborah Kerr, that was only an okay good movie, but it was, it was suspenseful especially the scene with the surprise villain trying to kill Deborah Kerr in scalding hot water in the bathtub. Mother, who I, who I saw it with, said it was Gary Cooper's last picture because he died and that was sad because she'd always liked Gary Cooper in the movies. Another interesting thing was that in 1961 I think I saw more black-and-white pictures than color pictures and that was another interesting thing.

Also, just to say it, just to have a record of it, I saw lots of movies that played with the Major Studio Previews and most of them I liked very much, and I also saw movies that weren't Major Studio Previews, that were just playing in theaters, but I'm only talking about Major Studio Previews because, because that's my life, that's what I live for, that's my reality.

Anyway, one day I, I went to the Village because anytime they, anytime they had a preview that's where I wanted to go even if there were other previews in other theaters, plus this one was an IMPORTANT Major Studio Preview in Technicolor. I don't remember, it's unusual for me, for me to, you know, for me to not remember but I don't remember what the movie was that was, that was playing there, but it doesn't really matter anyway.

I got there and got my ticket at the box office and the, the box office person said hi to me because as the manager had told me, I'd become a fixture there, a fixture at the Village and I liked that I was a fixture at the Village. The ticket taker at the door waved and said hi when he took my ticket and the lady behind the candy counter said hi and she already had a box of Dots out because I, because I was a fixture there and always had a box of Dots, and the usher said hi and called me Preview Harvey and then I, I found the seat I liked and sat down.

By the time the IMPORTANT Major Studio Preview began, the theater was totally full including the balcony upstairs. I never sat in the, in the balcony upstairs, I was never even *in* the balcony upstairs because heights made me nervous like James Stewart in *Vertigo*. Anyway, the whole, the whole theater was full. The lights went down and the curtains opened and the first thing we saw was the Paramount mountain so it was a Paramount Picture. Then a cab was coming down the street, which was empty, the street was empty and it, and it looked like early in the morning before people were up, and the music that played was, I didn't really understand it, even though it had only been a few seconds, the music that played was, the music that played was so beautiful and I was already hooked even though nothing had happened.

Anyway, the cab stopped in front of a store and a woman got out of the cab and the, and the woman was dressed up like going to a party or something, but she was in front of a building and looked up and saw a sign that said Tiffany's but nobody in the audience, including, including me, knew who the woman was because, because she had her back to us but then it said her name, Audrey Hepburn and everyone clapped, and I remembered her, I remembered her right away from, from *Roman Holiday* the first movie I saw with, with a, with my very first Major Studio Preview in the same theater I was in right now.

Then the title of the movie came on, *Breakfast at Tiffany's* and that beautiful music just kept getting more, getting more beautiful, and when they finally showed Audrey Hepburn's face, well, she looked, she looked, she looked different than in *Roman Holiday*. She was cute in *Roman Holiday* but I didn't want to marry her or anything, but now she was so beautiful that she, that she took my breath away and of course I wanted to marry her and I loved the movie, every second of it. Oh, and it was, it was directed by Blake Edwards, the man who I talked to outside the Village after *High Time*.

The movie had everything, big laughs, especially Mickey Rooney as a Japanese man, he was funny, it had a funny party scene, it had moving scenes, but it was, it was the ending, it was the ending with the rain and finding the cat named Cat and Audrey Hepburn and George Peppard kissing in the rain, holding the cat named Cat and I, I, I, wanted to be George Peppard kissing Audrey Hepburn in the, in the rain but I wasn't George Peppard, I was 5'3" Preview Harvey who'd never kissed anyone or had a cat named Cat or anything else and I don't know why but, I don't know why but there were tears running down my face and it's hard to tell this on the cassette but I have to, I just have to make a record of it because that feeling was, that feeling was so, that feeling was so overwhelming.

After the movie, I just had to sit in the, to sit in my seat for a few minutes, because I, because I didn't want to have tears running down my face for everyone to see, but, by the way, other people were sniffling too, I mean, I wasn't the only one sniffling with tears running down my face. Anyway, I, I finally got up and used the men's room and then went outside. Of course, I wondered if Audrey Hepburn was there but, but as far as I could see, she wasn't. The Paramount man was there, though, and he, he saw me and came over to me and said well, what did you think and I said it was maybe the best movie I'd ever seen and he smiled and I told him I thought it was going to be a big hit and that I'd be seeing it over and over and over again. He said just between you and me and the projection booth, it opens on October 18th at the Chinese.

Then out of the blue he, he took my arm, he took my arm and walked me over to a group of people and I, and I recognized Blake Edwards right away from the year before and the man said Blake, look who's here, Preview Harvey, you remember him from the *High Time* preview. Blake Edwards looked at me and shook my hand and said Preview Harvey, what a perfect name. Did you like the picture? I'm, I'm afraid I gushed like that oil gusher in that movie, in that movie *Giant*, and I said in my yakky way, I said Mr. Edwards I think it's the best movie I've ever seen and I loved it, everything, and I can't, I can't wait to see it again.

That got a big smile out of him and he said you're gonna be my good luck charm. He turned to the, to the Paramount man and said make sure you get Preview Harvey passes to the opening day at the Chinese, and the Paramount man said he would and then Blake Edwards thanked me for my kind words. The Paramount man walked me away and he, he gave me his card and said to call him and he'd arrange for the passes.

I told mother all about it when I, when I got home and she said she wished she'd gone with me, but I told her, I told her we could all go to see it after I got off work, we could all meet at the Chinese Theater and see it because I was getting, I was getting free passes from the Paramount man and that Blake Edwards told me I was going to be his, his good luck charm.

Oh, good, I, I, finished that story just in, just in the nick of time because the cassette is running out of tape now so I'll, I'll be back soon.

CASSETTE FOUR

Testing, testing.

I guess maybe I can stop, maybe I don't have to say testing testing anymore because, well, it works, the cassette machine works so why say testing testing anymore?

Anyway, we did go to the Chinese on October 18th and the Paramount man did get us passes that were under the name Preview Harvey at the box-office, and the audience reaction was even better than it had been at the, at the Village, and it was completely sold out and mother loved it as much as I did and she sniffled and had tears running down her face at the ending just like I did. Father just, father just sat there for most of it, but he did laugh every time Mickey Rooney was on the screen. He didn't understand why mother and I were sniffling at the end and had tears running down our faces and mother called him a dried-up old Fig Newton.

It played at the Chinese till December 11th and I saw it three more times there, right after work and my favorite, my favorite time I saw it it was raining like in the movie. The album of *Breakfast at Tiffany's* was our number one selling album at Wallichs Music City and we, we could barely keep it in stock, especially towards Christmas. I bought it the day it came out and I, I listened to it all the time, especially that music I loved, "Moon River." I was sad that it, that it didn't have the music from the kissing in the rain scene at the end but it had "Moon River," so I was fine.

Anyway, on November 22nd, I went to an IMPORTANT Major Studio Preview at the, at the gala re-opening of the new luxurious Lido Theater, which wasn't that far from us on Rexford in fake Beverly Hills. I'd never been to that theater and was, I was surprised to see how small it was and while it was okay inside, I didn't really see the luxurious part, but, but then again, maybe, maybe it had been not so luxurious before it was luxurious.

The IMPORTANT Major Studio preview at the new luxurious Lido was called *Bachelor Flat* and I could not have, I could not have have been happier because Tuesday Weld was in it and the guy who, the guy who played the lead, he had a weird name, Terry-Thomas, was so funny and had a big gap between his two front teeth that made me laugh every time he opened his mouth. And it was, it was directed by Frank Tashlin who made those two movies I liked so much with the fake Marilyn Monroe, Jayne Mansfield, you know, *The Girl Can't Help It* and *Will Success Spoil Rock Hunter?* and I hadn't, I hadn't seen anything he directed since *Will Success Spoil Rock Hunter?* and that was, that was in 1957. I laughed and laughed at *Bachelor Flat* and Tuesday Weld was still adorable and there was a funny dog carrying around a big bone too.

In December, we, we celebrated Christmas even though we were atheists. We had a big Christmas tree with lights and ornaments and I, I liked Christmas because it was, it was festive and we, we always exchanged presents. I bought mother a pair of, I bought her a pair of Christian Dior Green Glass clip-on earrings. Mother loved them and she, she put them on and said I shouldn't have wasted the money on her and I said it wasn't a waste, wasn't a waste at all because she deserved a nice new pair of earrings.

I got father a new cologne called Messire eau de toilette by Jean d'Albret. I, I didn't really, I didn't really know about colognes, but mother had whispered to me more than, she'd whispered to me more than once that father would smell when he got home from work, well, she called it rank and he could, he could use some cologne so he wouldn't, so he wouldn't smell up the house and the, and the person at the department store said this was a, this was a nice cologne.

When father opened it, he, he looked at the bottle and read it in his, in his monotone monotonous voice and pronounced "toilette" as "toilet" and said so this is toilet water? I could have just gotten it out of the toilet, why spend good money on it? Mother had to explain to him what it was, that "toilette" didn't literally mean water in the toilet bowl, and then he, he opened the bottle and smelled it and said this smells lemony, you want me to smell like a lemon and, and mother said that's better than smelling like a sewer, and mother and I laughed, and father said ha, ha, ha, you're regular comedians, then he, then he put some on and it, it did smell lemony.

They got me several presents. I got a red pullover sweater and I, and I put it right on and it, it fit and looked good, at least that's, that's what mother said. Father thought I, thought I looked like a little tomato in it. I also got a reserved seat ticket to see, to see the new roadshow movie that replaced

Breakfast at Tiffany's at the, at the Chinese, a 70mm picture called *West Side Story*. As far as I knew, they never, they never had Major Studio Previews of 70mm roadshow movies so I was excited to see it since I'd, I'd already seen a few roadshow movies like *Exodus* and *Can-Can*. They also got me five boxes of, of Dots for the house and that was a, a good present.

So, that was a, that was a nice Christmas. On New Year's Eve they had Major Studio Previews everywhere, in a whole bunch of theaters, probably all the, all the same movie because it was all in Fox West Coast Theater theaters and I, I didn't like to be driving on New Year's Eve because, because mother had put the fear of God into me about drunk drivers and horrible car crash accidents and people's heads going through windshields. So I, so I stayed home and we, we watched a movie on television on channel nine and you won't, you won't believe what the movie was so I'll tell you it was *The High and The Mighty*, that was, that was the movie and I hadn't seen it since 1954 but on TV it wasn't in Cinemascope or color and there were, there were a lot of scenes missing and they kept stopping it for commercials and it just wasn't, it just wasn't the same at all, even though John Wayne still whistled at the end.

At midnight, we shouted Happy New Year and had a toast. I had a glass of, of Coca-Cola, mother had a cup of tea, and father had, father had made a piece of toast because he thought it was funny if he made a toast with toast. And then, and then, suddenly it was, it was 1962.

The first interesting thing in 1962 didn't have a thing to do with Major Studio Previews, it had to do with the, with the coincidence that on January 10th, *Breakfast at Tiffany's* opened everywhere and so did *Bachelor Flat*. What, what were the, what were the chances of that happening? I saw *Breakfast at Tiffany's* nine times, three at the Wiltern Theater, which wasn't too far from, from Wallichs Music City, well, I mean, it wasn't that close but it wasn't too far and the Wiltern was a beautiful movie palace, and then six times at the Picwood. I saw *Bachelor Flat* two more times, both at the Bruin in Westwood, right across from, right across from the Village. That was my first time at the Bruin, but it wasn't nearly as nice a theater as, as the Village was.

I went to a lot of Major Studio Previews in 1962 but I also went to some previews that didn't say Major Studio and I, and I hadn't been to one of those kinds since, since *Target Earth* in 1954. Also, in 1962, I don't know, movies seemed, movies seemed to be changing or maybe I was changing, it might have been I was changing and liking new kinds of, new kinds of movies, that could have been it.

But before I, before I get to all that and the Major Studio Previews and other previews, first I want to tell about, about the biggest change in 1962 because it was a big change and one that made me, that made me very nervous and anxious but mother said it was, it was time, I was turning twenty-two and it was time, and Mother Knows Best, that was, that was what we said in our almost house on Rexford.

So, in July of 1962, I moved, I moved into my own apartment and it, it made me nervous and anxious at least at, at least at the beginning until I, until I finally got used to being there, alone, and then, then I knew Mother Knows Best because out of the blue I liked it, liked living alone, being by myself in my, in my own little space. Besides, it was, it was only, it was only a five-minute drive to our almost house on Rexford in fake Beverly Hills so I could see mother and father anytime I, anytime I wanted.

My apartment was on South Holt Avenue, south of Olympic right up the, right up the street from that little new luxurious Lido Theater where I'd seen the preview of *Bachelor Flat*.

It was, it was a, I think mother called it, she called it a studio or efficiency apartment. 550-square feet they told mother. Just one room, a little, a little kitchen, a closet, and a, you know, and a bathroom. We, we brought over my bed and dresser and mother and father bought a, they bought a new couch and I, I got the old couch and the, and the chair that went, the chair that went with it. I had my, I had my record player, and my clothes in the closet, mother gave me some dishes and silverware, and I had a, I had my own parking space too.

The rent was eighty dollars a month and I was, I was making $200 a month, thanks to the raise and minimum wage going up, so, so mother said that seemed okay and I'd, I'd have enough left over for, for food and movies. Father thought that we were all going to the poorhouse anyway, so, so what did, what did any of it matter.

Anyway, I, I felt like a, like a real adult and my little efficiency or studio apartment suited me fine and it still suits me fine because I'm still in it although it's a little, a little cluttery now. Mother said I had to have a telephone and she'd pay for it. I didn't, I didn't really care about a telephone, but she insisted so she could, so she could call me when she needed to and I could call her when I needed to and in case there was, in case there was an emergency, heaven forbid. So, I had, I had my own phone and, and my own phone number. At first, mother called all the time to tell me, to tell me she missed me something terrible but I, but I reminded her that it was her idea and Mother Knows Best and she'd laugh and tell me I wasn't her baby anymore, I was her big boy out on his, out on his own, well not big, no one was ever, was ever going to mistake me for big.

I had dinner at the almost house on Rexford twice a week, so it's not like, it's not like I didn't see them all the time.

Father didn't say much, he seemed, I don't know, he seemed, he seemed a little, a little far away, but I did notice he smelled lemony so he was using the Messire eau de toilette I got him for Christmas.

Anyway, that was, that was the big event of, of 1962. Basically, well, basically my life was just working at Wallichs Music City until five then going to a Major Studio Preview at one of my, at one of my favorite theaters or sometimes even, sometimes even a new theater, and I'd see Nate Fahr at a lot of the Major Studio Previews and we'd, we'd talk about movies and what we liked and didn't like but the most important thing was, the most important thing was that we noticed a couple of others were showing up regularly at Major Studio Previews and we, we met them and Joe and Gary were their names and they were preview nuts like we were preview nuts and we became, we became like a little, a little club, not friends, but just people who loved and were fixated on Major Studio Previews.

We saw some amazing Major Studio Previews that year, but, but like I said, some of them were very, some of them were very different and I began to really like the movies that were, the movies that were different and like the year before, I saw a lot of, a lot of black-and-white movies. And besides the Village I began to be, I began to be known at other theaters and was greeted there by people who, by people who worked there and who called me Preview Harvey.

The first preview I saw in 1962 was called *Light in the Piazza* and I liked that one because it had the girl from *Where the Boys Are* and *The Time Machine*, Yvette Mimieux, and she was so fragile and pretty and of course I, I added her to the list of girls I wanted to marry. She played a girl with, well, I guess you'd say a girl with a condition so I commiserated with her because, you know, just because. I saw that one at the

Culver Theater in Culver City and I'd never been there but it was right near M-G-M Studios and *Light in the Piazza* was an M-G-M picture. When the title had come on, I thought it had said *Light in the Pizza* and that was confusing but thankfully it wasn't a movie about a pizza.

At the Picwood, that was, that was another theater where they, where they knew me and called me Preview Harvey, and at the Picwood I saw *The Road to Hong Kong* with Bing Crosby and Bob Hope and I'd seen some other *Road* pictures with them on TV and liked them and I guess I, I guess I sort of liked this one, but Bob Hope and Bing Crosby looked, they looked, well, they looked old and tired and bored, but there were surprise cameos in it, like Frank Sinatra and Dean Martin and the, and the original *Road* girl, Dorothy Lamour, but the only really funny thing in it that made me really laugh was a man named, a man named Peter Sellers who had one scene but got the biggest laughs in the picture.

In early March, I was, I was back at the Village for an IMPORTANT Major Studio Preview and everyone said hi to me and was happy to see me, that's what they said, it was my first preview at the Village that year. Nate and Joe and Gary were there and we talked before the movie and then found our own special seats and I of course had my Dots, I was never without my Dots.

The curtains opened and the IMPORTANT Major Studio Preview began with the Columbia Pictures torch lady in black-and-white and really creepy music that made me, that made me nervous. Then it said A Blake Edwards Production and I couldn't believe it, my, my third Blake Edwards preview at the Village Theater. I wondered if Mr. Edwards was in the audience and if I'd, you know, if I'd get to talk to him after the movie.

Glenn Ford and Lee Remick's names were next and I remembered her from that movie *Anatomy of a Murder* and then the, the title of the movie came on, *Experiment in Terror.* I didn't like scary movies but it was Blake Edwards so I knew it would be, I knew it would be a good picture and it was a really good picture. You could have, you could have heard a pin drop it was, it was so quiet in the theater and the villain was so creepy with his raspy asthma breathing and so nasty and mean to, mean to Lee Remick and especially to her sister, who I'd never seen before.

And that music was so, it was so, it was so creepy and disturbing and it was by my, my favorite movie composer Henry Mancini, because he did the music for *High Time* and *Breakfast at Tiffany's* and *The Great Impostor* too. The thing that was, the thing that was interesting was that someone who made such funny, colorful movies, could make such a creepy and scary movie. Anyway, the ending was, it was very exciting and the audience applauded when it said The End. I couldn't wait to see it again.

I talked to my, my fellow preview nuts for a bit, and then walked outside. It was, I remember it was chilly and thankfully I had on my red sweater from Christmas so it wasn't, it wasn't too bad. Before I could, before I could even look around to see if any of the actors were there, I heard a voice say there he is, there's Preview Harvey, my good luck charm and Mr. Edwards was walking towards me. He said did you like it and I said Mr. Edwards, I don't, I don't know, I don't know how you do it but you outdid yourself and it was, it was so, it was so different from your other movies. He smiled and said I guess that means we have the Preview Harvey seal of approval and then he said come meet some people. I know that Nate and Joe and Gary were watching, were watching this happen, and their, their mouths were practically touching the floor.

Mr. Edwards took me to the group he was with and said this is my good luck charm, Preview Harvey. He's seen my last two pictures when they previewed here and tonight we got the Preview Harvey seal of approval and that, my friends, is good enough for me and good enough to take to the bank.

Oh, you're wondering how I, you may be wondering how I, how I remember what he said, well, as soon as I got back to the car I, I wrote it down in my notebook. That's what I, that's what I always did even though I have a really, a really good memory for everything, I wrote everything down in a notebook so I could, so I could remember things, which is why I can, you know, why I can make a record of things on these cassette tapes.

Mr. Edwards patted me on the top of, on the top of my head, well, on the top of my Hollywood Stars baseball cap and said Preview Harvey these are some people from Columbia and I can tell you that they're thrilled to have the Preview Harvey seal of approval because that's a good omen and means the picture's going to perform well. He looked at the people from Columbia and said hear that fellas? They laughed, and then Mr. Edwards said oh, and this is our star, Lee Remick. I turned to who he was talking about and there was Lee Remick, she'd, she'd been standing in back of someone, but there was Lee Remick who was so good in the movie and if I, if I thought she was pretty in the movies, she was, she was, indescribable in person, so beautiful, with, with eyes bluer than a, than a Technicolor blue sky. She said nice to meet you, Preview Harvey, is it? I said that's what Jerry Lewis called me when I saw his movie previewed at the Village and now it's what everyone calls me. She said why and I said because I go to all the Major Studio Previews and I have since I was, since I was fourteen. She said well, keep going, we need people like you, we really do.

I didn't, I didn't, I never wanted to overstay my, my welcome and I didn't know, I didn't know what else to say so I said goodnight to everyone and as I, as I headed to my car, Nate and Joe and Gary ran up to me and said how amazing it was I got to talk to Mr. Edwards and Lee Remick. And it, it was amazing and I, I wrote it all down the second I got in the car. When I got home, I called mother and told her and she was, she was amazed too.

So, I already, I already thought 1962 was my, was the, the best year so far just because of all the interesting things and also because there were, there were so many good Major Studio Previews that were, that I loved. Okay, so maybe, so maybe you noticed, maybe you noticed I pretty much love almost every Major Studio Preview but not all Major Studio Previews and I haven't, you know, I haven't really talked about the stinkers much because, like I already said, why, what's the point but just in case here is an example of a, of a Major Studio Preview that I saw in 1962 that was a stinker, just so no one thinks that I, that I don't love, I mean that I love every single Major Studio Preview that I see.

The Major Studio Preview that was a stinker was called *I Thank a Fool*, an M-G-M picture in Cinemascope and Metrocolor. First of all, first of all, I didn't like Metrocolor to begin with, it didn't, it wasn't like Technicolor or even Color by Deluxe, it looked, it looked drab and didn't, I don't know, it didn't, it was drab, at least I thought it was drab and I didn't care for it, so that was one thing I didn't love right off the, right off the bat. The movie was drab too and Susan Hayward was the star and I'd never seen her before and I thought, I thought why doesn't she ever smile, she's always frowning and she's, she's a doctor and kills a patient at the start of the movie, they call it a mercy killing but she goes to jail for two years for the mercy killing but not like Monopoly jail, real jail, then she gets out of jail and goes to work for the man who put her in jail and she, she frowns some more and then I couldn't keep track of who was doing what and why they were doing it and who they were doing it to, but I, I stayed till the end and everything was explained and I still didn't understand it and when mother asked how I liked the movie I told her it was a stinker.

So, see, that was, that was an example of a stinker but I just don't like to talk about the stinkers as much as I, as much as I like talking about the ones I do like. Mother always said that you can catch more flies with honey than with vinegar and even though I didn't like flies because of that movie *The Fly*, I liked honey more than vinegar because vinegar smelled.

So, here are, here are some other Major Studio Previews I loved in 1962. *The Man Who Shot Liberty Valance*, a Paramount Picture with John Wayne and James Stewart, two of my favorites and it was, it was a western with a really mean villain named Liberty Valance and it was in black-and-white and I, I thought it was great and told the man from Paramount that it was great. *Mr. Hobbs Takes a Vacation* in Cinemascope and color, that one was at the Village and had James Stewart in it again and so of course I loved it and it was funny and I liked the lady in it, Maureen O'Hara, who had red hair the exact color, the exact color of my red sweater I got for Christmas. I was, I was hoping that maybe James Stewart was at the preview but he wasn't, but this young guy who was in the movie, Fabian, he was there and I, I wasn't that interested in talking to Fabian and besides he was, he was surrounded by teenage girls who probably would have killed me if I'd, if I'd tried to butt in and anyway the only thing I could think of to ask him was why do you only have one name?

At the Picwood, I saw two Major Studio Previews in black-and-white that were, that were really, I guess the word would be powerful, really powerful. The first was called *Requiem for a Heavyweight* with Anthony Quinn, Jackie Gleason, and Mickey Rooney, not playing a Japanese man and not being funny, nothing was funny in *Requiem for a Heavyweight* and it was about a, about a washed up boxer and it was so gritty and real and the music was great and I was, I was really liking these new kinds of movies. But if I, but if I thought that was gritty the other one I saw at the Picwood, *Pressure Point*, with Sidney Poitier and Bobby Darin, well, that was, that one was kind of, kind of creepy and disturbing and I'd, I'd, I'd never seen anything like it before because it had weird dream scenes that were, that were really creepy and I really liked Sidney Poitier and I only knew that Bobby Darin sang "Splish Splash" and I had no idea he was such a good actor, playing a terrible awful creepy and disturbing person. I saw both movies again when they, when they were released.

I saw some others, some Major Studio Previews that were very good, but the two best ones, two of the best ones were *The Manchurian Candidate* with Frank Sinatra and another actor I didn't know, Laurence Harvey, and another beautiful girl, Leslie Parrish and I wanted to marry her. Anyway, it was, it was another movie that wasn't like any other movie I'd seen. It was weird and was about a brainwashed person and I didn't know what that meant until that movie, and it was another creepy and disturbing movie and had the weirdest scene I'd ever seen in a, in a movie, where Laurence Harvey's mother kisses him on the lips not very much like a mother should kiss a son, not like that, that was creepy and disturbing but the whole movie was creepy and disturbing but I, I couldn't take my eyes off the screen, not even for a minute, not even to see what color Dots I was eating.

Oh, and it was in black-and-white and it seemed like all the Major Studio Previews that I loved that year were in black-and-white and I couldn't stop talking about *The Manchurian Candidate* and I made mother and father come with me to see it when it, when it came out and mother loved it as much as I did, and I'm not sure what father thought because he, because he fell asleep halfway through it and woke up just before the ending and said loudly, what did I miss? Anyway, that Major Studio Preview was at the, that Major Studio Preview was at the Bay Theater on Sunset Boulevard in Pacific Palisades and I'd never heard of that theater or Pacific Palisades. It was a, it was a long drive but worth all the gas it cost and I wasn't, I wasn't worried like father that I'd end up in the poorhouse.

But the best, the best one, the one that really, I don't know, really got me was back at the Village, another IMPORTANT Major Studio Preview. It didn't say in Cinemascope or color and VistaVision, VistaVision seemed to have, it seemed to have disappeared because I hadn't seen a, a VistaVision credit on a Paramount movie since *One-Eyed Jacks*. Anyway, anyway I figured it would be another black-and-white movie. I got there and everyone said hi to me and Nate was there and so were, and so were Joe and Gary.

Wait, I don't think I said much about Joe and Gary but I didn't really know them so there isn't, there isn't much to say, other than Joe was always dressed in a suit and tie, I mean the same suit and tie, he always wore the same suit and tie, maybe he only had one suit and tie, and he was skinny as a stick and his hair was always, his hair was always, his hair looked like it had too much stuff in it, stuff, you know, stuff like Brylcreem or stuff like that, it was slick and greasy-looking and I didn't ever want to put stuff in my hair not that I had much hair by that point and no one saw it anyway because of my Hollywood Stars baseball cap. Joe always got buttered popcorn, I never, I never saw him without his buttered popcorn and he said he always got two squirts of butter on it. Anyway, Gary was the opposite of Joe, he was, he was, he was chubby and wore khaki pants with his stomach hanging over them and his shirts always seemed to, always seemed to have stains, like food had dripped on his shirt or something. That was Joe and Gary.

See, I did it again. I was, I was talking about the IMPORTANT Major Studio Preview at the Village, but then I, I, I switched to something else like a Mexican jumping bean, because that's what happens because, well, I said that already about how my brain works so let me get back to, to what I was talking about.

Anyway, anyway, Nate and I were yakky and then Joe and Gary came and we all talked until it was time for the movie to start. This time, Gary had a, he had a big green stain on his, on his white shirt and I finally just asked him about it because I, I have no off button. Gary said I'm so glad you asked me about that, it's Andersen's pea soup. He said he was one of those kids who always got food on his shirts so he, so he began making the stains into art by, by adding to them and that he'd made the Andersen's pea soup green stain into an art shape he called Green Dragon in the Snow. Then we all sat in our seats.

The lights went down and the curtain opened and yes, it was, it was in black-and-white and had the Warner Bros. shield thing and bcautiful music was playing and then it said Jack Lemmon and everyone clapped and of course I, I loved Jack Lemmon especially from *Mister Roberts* and *Some Like It Hot*, and then it said Lee Remick and I was so happy because I'd met Lee Remick at *Experiment in Terror* and I, I only wished whatever the movie was was in color so I could see those Technicolor blue sky eyes again, and I already guessed that the music was by Henry Mancini, my favorite, because it just sounded like his music and I guess it could have been someone else but I was sure it was Henry Mancini, then then there was singing as the movie title came up, a chorus was singing the movie title *Days of Wine and Roses*, and I didn't know what that meant but the song was so haunting and beautiful that I knew I was going to love the movie because Lee Remick and Jack Lemmon were in it.

I didn't recognize any of the other actor names, and then it said the song was by Johnny Mercer and Henry Mancini and then it said Music by Henry Mancini so I was right about Henry Mancini, and then the final credit came up and it was, it was Directed by Blake Edwards. I couldn't, I couldn't believe it, another Blake Edwards Major Studio Preview in the same, in the same year at the Village, that must have been his, his favorite theater to have his Major Studio Previews and I, I, I was sure he was in the audience. Anyway, the movie was amazing, about two people who, who drink too much, and Jack Lemmon was nothing like, nothing like the funny Jack Lemmon I'd seen before, he was a frightening and scary Jack Lemmon when he was drunk and he was drunk in the movie a lot and he got Lee Remick to be drunk too and she got worse, she got worse than him and she was, she was so good and the music was, was so good, and everything was, everything was so good.

Anyway, after it was over everyone clapped and I clapped too, probably, probably louder than anyone. After the curtains closed, Nate and Joe and Gary and I talked about how great it was and then I said goodbye to them and walked outside to the front of the theater and looked around and sure enough Mr. Edwards was there with his, with his group of people. They were standing off to the, off to the side so people wouldn't, you know, wouldn't crowd around them, they always stood off to the side but I knew where they stood from the other times they were there, so I, I knew where they'd be.

I worked my way over to where they were and stood off to the side, waiting for a chance to tell Mr. Edwards what I thought. One of the people tapped him on the, on the shoulder and pointed at me and Mr. Edwards turned around and he saw me standing there waiting and he, he smiled a big smile and said look who's here, my good luck charm, Preview Harvey, come over here. I came over there and he shook my, he shook my hand and said what is this, the fourth preview of mine you've seen? I said yes, fourth one, and this one, this one was the best, and I don't know, I don't know how you make so many different kinds of movies but this one was the best and I loved everything about it, all the, all the scenes and everything about it and I'm sorry for being yakky but I just, I just thought this was the best.

Mr. Edwards laughed and said yakky? I've never heard that word before. I said mother always says I'm a motormouth and yakky. I wished I had an off button because I was just blabbering now, but Mr. Edwards seemed to find it funny so maybe I was funny and he said I have to find a way to use yakky in a movie. I couldn't believe he said that and I thought, I thought wouldn't that be something if he used yakky in a movie. He said to his group I think some of you have met Preview Harvey before, and you know, he hasn't been wrong yet, every time he says we have a hit we have a hit and he's batting a thousand.

I didn't know what batting a thousand meant, but I, I think it was a good thing. I said I think this one is going to be a big hit. Oh and I, and I loved the music by Mr. Mancini, he's my favorite too.

Mr. Edwards said he's my favorite too, that's why he scores all my movies. He turned to a tall man in his group, a tall man with about as much hair as I had, which wasn't much and he said Hank, meet Preview Harvey, he thinks you're the best and you are. Whoever Hank was stepped forward and shook my hand and said Henry Mancini and I'm so pleased you like my music. I was, I was, I couldn't, I was shaking hands with Henry Mancini, my favorite, and I didn't, I didn't know what I should say so I just, I just said I love your music and I have all your records because I work at Wallichs Music City and I tell everyone to buy your records. Mr. Mancini smiled and said well, every sale helps the cause, and then he laughed.

Then I, I did something I've, I did something I'd never done before, I, I, took out a piece of paper and a pen and said to Mr. Edwards I've never done this before but would you sign this paper? Mr. Edwards said I'd be delighted to sign it. He took the paper and pen and wrote something and, and he signed it, then I, then I said Mr. Mancini would you sign it too and he said of course I will and he signed it too and they handed me back the paper and pen. I thanked them both and then I, I said how great the picture was again and then, and then I thought it was a good time to leave and I left.

When I got back to the car, my, my hands were shaking as I, as I turned on the inside car light and looked at the paper they'd signed. Mr. Edwards had written, "To my lucky charm, Preview Harvey, don't ever lose your enthusiasm! With affection, Blake Edwards." And below it, below it Mr. Mancini had written, "It makes a composer very happy to know that people actually hear the music in a movie and for that I am eternally grateful. Henry Mancini." I must've sat there for thirty minutes reading it over and over again and I felt, I felt, I felt like the, like the, well, as mother puts it, like the cat who got the cream.

When I got home, I called mother even though it was late. Luckily, she wasn't asleep she was watching the television news with Clete Roberts, I mean, she wasn't watching the news *with* Clete Roberts, I mean Clete Roberts was, was on the, on the news and she was watching it. She said did you see a preview tonight? I said yes a great movie called *Days of Wine and Roses* with Jack Lemmon and Lee Remick from *Anatomy of a Murder* and *Experiment in Terror* and the movie was about people who, who drank too much, not a comedy a drama and you'll never, you'll never guess who directed it and who was there, you'll, you'll, never guess in a million zillion years. She said slow down and take a breath already and if I won't guess then tell me who was there. I said Blake Edwards. She said again? How many movies does he make a year and I said well, well, two this year for sure. This is, this is the fourth movie of his I've seen at an IMPORTANT Major Studio Preview at the Village but that's not the best thing.

She said what's the best thing? I said the best thing was, the best thing was Mr. Edwards was there again, like all the other times. She said that's wonderful, did you talk to him? I said yes, and that was the best thing. I told him I loved the movie and thought it was going to be a big hit and that I loved the music, the music was so beautiful and haunting and he, and he, you won't believe it, he introduced me to a man, a tall man without much, without much hair, and he called the man Hank and Hank, you won't believe it, and Hank was Henry Mancini, you know, Henry Mancini who writes the music for all of Mr. Edwards' movies but that's not the best thing, that's not the bcst thing at all.

She said Hahveeeeee you're going to give yourself a heart attack. Take a breath and tell me what the best thing was. I took a breath and told her they'd both signed a paper, signed it to me personally, Preview Harvey, and they wrote beautiful things. She said read it to me, I want to hear what they wrote. I read it to her and she was, she said she was going to cry because what they wrote was so beautiful. She said you take care of that paper and come over and bring it and I'll get it framed for you and you can hang it on the wall.

That was a great idea and I couldn't wait to bring it to her so she could, so she could get it framed and I could hang it on the wall because I didn't have anything on the wall and now I would. We got off the phone and I brushed my teeth and got in bed but I couldn't fall asleep because I had the, I had the light on and kept reading the paper over and over again because I was fixated on it and couldn't stop.

Then about seven days later, it was, it was, you know, it was hanging on the wall and I can't think of a day when I didn't stop to, when I didn't stop to look at it. It's still there and I still look at it every day. Well, the cassette is running out of tape and I'm exhausted because talking this much in a row is, is exhausting especially when you're yakky and a motormouth. Anyway, I'm out of cassettes so tomorrow, tomorrow at work I'll buy more cassettes and then, and then I, can continue making a, a record of things on cassettes.

CASSETTE FIVE

Okay, I'm, I'm back with more cassettes and I'm not exhausted anymore so, so here I go again. I just, I just want to say that making this record is, is interesting and it's, it's fun to look back and remember all these things, all these, all these things and thank goodness I have a good memory and good lists to look at.

Anyway, we're almost through with 1962 and the, the more I remember the more I, the more I think that was the best year for Major Studio Previews or at least one of the best even though there were, there were other great years, including 1963 and I'll talk about 1963 but, but I haven't really finished with 1962 because, because more interesting things happened so I'll start with the, I'll start where I, where I left off, I think where I left off was *Days of Wine and Roses* so I guess, I guess I'll start from there.

First, first before I, before I forget, when *Days of Wine and Roses* finally opened two months later, it was, it was in Hollywood at the, at the Vogue Theater not that far from Wallichs Music City. Anyway, it opened at the, at the Vogue on December 25th, Christmas Day and I thought, I thought that was weird to start a movie about people who, people who drink too much on Christmas Day because first of all who went to movies on Christmas Day, not even I went to movies on Christmas Day because it was Christmas Day and that was for, you know, opening presents and stuff like that, even for atheists. But it said in the advertisement, it said an interesting thing and that was interesting the interesting thing. It said Pre-Release in Order to Qualify for Academy Award Consideration with an, with an exclamation point after Consideration. I don't know why, really, but I, but I never paid much attention to the Academy Awards but now I wanted to pay attention and see, and see what got nominated, just to see how many movies I loved got, you know, got nominated.

Anyway, I thought that was interesting that it opened on Christmas Day because it wasn't exactly a, a movie filled with, with holiday cheer. But, but my, my point is, my point is that I was now fixated on the Academy Awards and what would get nominated and win. The other thing was I couldn't wait to get the album of *Days of Wine and Roses* so I could play it over and over again, but we didn't get it at Wallichs Music City before Christmas and when I asked Nametag Walter about it, he, he looked in the new releases for the big Phonolog Catalog and said, he said he didn't see it.

After Christmas Day, I went back, I went back to work and we still didn't have any *Days of Wine and Roses* album and it still wasn't listed and I didn't understand it and it never did come out and I never did understand it. We did finally get a 45, a 45 of the song with a nice picture sleeve and that was by Henry Mancini like it was in the movie, so I bought that and played it over and over again and the interesting thing that happened the week that I got the 45, the interesting thing that happened was that they were painting the outside of the apartment building where I, where I lived, and I could, you know, I could, I could smell the paint inside my apartment while I was playing the 45 and even when I play the song now and I still play it and my other Henry Mancini records, even when I play it now I can, I can still smell the paint smell and that's interesting, at least to me it is.

Anyway, the last Major Studio Previews I saw in 1962 were, they were all very different. For one of them, there was, there was an ad in the paper and it said, it said something I'd never seen before, it said, it said Gala Major Studio Preview Year's Funniest Comedy. So. of course I, I had to be there for the Year's Funniest Comedy and to find out what Gala meant. It was at the Wilshire, which was on Wilshire, not so far from where mother and father lived on Rexford in fake Beverly Hills. Before I went, I had dinner with mother and father. It was, it was nice to have a, you know, it was nice to have a home cooked meal rather than my usual homemade Swiss cheese sandwiches on Weber's Bread. I can't, I can't remember what she made and I, I didn't write it down but whatever it was it was good because mother is a very good cook no matter what she makes.

They didn't want to go the Gala Major Studio Preview The Year's Funniest Comedy because father had worked overtime at his job and was tired and mother, mother had dishes to do and just wanted to stay home. So, I went and got there just as the movie that was, that was playing there, *Hemingway's Adventures of a Young Man*, finished. I managed to get a seat, not my usual seat, but a good seat, and Nate, Joe, and Gary were there and came and said hi and we talked until it was time for the movie to start. I still didn't know what Gala meant, I mean there was nothing different about this preview than any other preview, I mean, whatever the Gala part was I didn't see it. Maybe the Gala part would be after the movie.

The Year's Funniest Comedy was called *If a Man Answers* and Sandra Dee and Bobby Darin were the stars and there's, there's not much to say about it other than I didn't, I didn't think it was The Year's Funniest Comedy, I thought it was okay good, not even good good. But the funny thing was that I, that I hadn't actually seen many Major Studio Previews that year that were, that were comedies, not like the years before 1962. But this one wasn't as, it wasn't as funny as *Bachelor Flat* or *Mr. Hobbs Takes a Vacation* so no, to me it wasn't The Year's Funniest Comedy. And it kind of got unfunnier, I think that's a word, it kind of got unfunnier as it, as it went on and that wasn't good for The Year's Funniest Comedy. Maybe in 1962 I just liked dramas and weird pictures better, maybe that's what it was. Sandra Dee was cute but I just kept seeing Bobby Darin the way he, the way he was in that movie *Pressure Point*, you know, as a really mean and disturbed person and once you'd seen him like that it was hard to, hard to think he was, well, that he was charming, because once you'd seen him be mean and disturbed you just kept thinking he was going to kill Sandra Dee or something. But that's because I saw *Pressure Point* before I saw The Year's Funniest Comedy, *If a Man Answers*. I don't, I don't think many other people went to see *Pressure Point* when it came out so maybe, maybe everyone else saw the charming Bobby Darin where I saw the, I saw the mean and disturbed Bobby Darin.

After The Year's Funniest Comedy was over, in the lobby, I talked to the other preview nuts and Gary said he kind of liked it and Joe thought it was, it was pretty funny and Nate said he didn't care for it much and I said I thought it was okay good and since this was, this was a Universal picture I was glad the Paramount guy wasn't there so I didn't have to tell him that it was only okay good. I never did figure out the Gala part, I mean no Gala people were there, at least that I could see, and they, they didn't serve finger sandwiches or have free drinks so as far as I was concerned that newspaper advertisement was fake because unless they hid the Gala part there was no Gala.

The last three, the last three Major Studio Previews I saw in 1962 were, were movies that were, well, they weren't like other movies from that year, at least ones I'd seen. The first one, the first one I saw was at the end of November, and the other two I saw in December. I won't spend too much time on two of them, even though I, I really liked them both, but I won't spend too much time on them because I want to spend time on the third one because, because that was the one, that was the one, well, I'll get to that one in a minute. So, the two in December were, well, one was something called an IMPORTANT Press Preview and I'd never seen a preview called a Press Preview and I asked mother what it meant and she thought it meant like the press, newspapers, you know, newspapers for reviews, like that press, and I'm sure, I'm sure she was right, so I went just because I wanted to attend an IMPORTANT Press Preview.

The IMPORTANT Press Preview was at a little theater on Wilshire in the, in the Miracle Mile, called the El Rey. It was kind of like that new luxurious Lido Theater where I saw *Bachelor Flat*, but without, you know, without the new luxurious part. Anyway, the, the movie was called *David and Lisa*, and it was about two people with mental problems who become friends and help each other with their mental problems and it was a very different kind of movie and I loved it. The girl spoke in rhymes and the boy didn't want to be touched, those were their mental problems. I guess, I guess you could call their mental problems conditions, you know, like my

That's Just Harvey condition, so I could, I could understand that part and I was just happy that my condition wasn't as bad as their condition so I didn't have to be in a home or an institution like they were. It seemed like a, like a small picture, not a big studio picture, just a small black-and-white picture, but I did love it and wanted to see it again and I thought, I thought all the actors were good even though I didn't know who any of them were. Another interesting thing was that it opened only four days after the preview, and just for one week, like *Days of Wine and Roses*, for Academy Award Consideration with an exclamation point, and that, that was interesting too because it wasn't, it didn't seem like a picture that would be up for Academy Awards, being such a small picture.

The other preview was just called an IMPORTANT Preview, and, and that one was at the Fine Arts on Wilshire just a few blocks from the Wilshire Theater on Wilshire. Anyway it was another black-and-white picture and it was called *The Trial* and it didn't, it didn't look like any other movie I'd ever seen. It was almost like a dream or something, I don't really, I don't really know how to describe it and I'm not sure I understood any of it other than the police show up at the apartment of someone and arrest him but they don't tell him what he did or why they're arresting him they just tell him there'll be a trial. The leading actor was Anthony Perkins and I, I hadn't seen any Major Studio Previews that he was in but I'd seen *Psycho* in 1960 because it was, it was playing with a Major Studio Preview I saw, and it scared the pants off me and I jumped out of my seat twice, which had never, which had never happened before.

Anyway, *The Trial* didn't scare the pants off me but it was creepy and weird looking and I didn't know what to, what to think of it, but I wanted to see it again so I could see if, you know, if I could understand it better and I did see it two more times and I never, I never understood it better other than it was weird and creepy and Anthony Perkins got dynamited at the end of the movie even though he said he wasn't, he wasn't guilty of anything, he still got dynamited at the end.

But the movie I saw at the end of November, that's the one, the one I really want to talk about because, well, because that's the one I became fixated on. That preview was called an IMPORTANT Foreign Preview and I'd never been to an IMPORTANT Foreign Preview either and I didn't know what it meant. I asked mother if she wanted to see an IMPORTANT Foreign Preview and she said no and, and she, she reminded me that we'd seen a foreign preview even though it, it wasn't called that, it was just called a Preview in color and that was *Come Dance with Me* with Brigitte Bardot, the movie mother thought was too racy but that I enjoyed anyway because I wanted to marry Brigitte Bardot. Anyway, mother didn't want to come to the IMPORTANT Foreign Preview because she thought it might be racy.

The IMPORTANT Foreign Preview was at the new luxurious Lido where I'd, where I'd seen *Bachelor Flat*. They were showing a picture called *Divorce, Italian Style* and it was in Italian with English writing at the bottom of the picture, you know, so you knew what they were saying. I only saw the last ten minutes of it, but I, I didn't see any of the actual picture because I was busy reading the writing at the bottom of the screen and I got, I got impatient reading and couldn't really concentrate, but people were laughing so I guess it was a, I guess it was a comedy.

When I went out to go buy Dots, I asked the ticket taker what kind of foreign preview it was. He couldn't, he couldn't tell me the name of it, of course, but he said it was a French movie and that it was, and that it was supposed to be great.

The IMPORTANT Foreign Preview began and it was in Cinemascope although it didn't say that, it said Franscope so it was in Franscope in black-and-white. The movie was called *Sundays and Cybele* and it had writing on the bottom of the screen too and everyone was speaking, I guess they were speaking in French, since it was a French picture. Obviously, I didn't know who any of the actors were. I tried to read the writing quickly so I could, so I could watch what was happening on the screen because it was so beautiful to look at in Franscope and black-and-white. It was about a guy who crashed in his airplane and then something was wrong with him after that and then one day, he sees a little girl with her father and her father is leaving his little girl at, at an orphanage and the little girl doesn't want to be left at an orphanage and she's sad and she's, she's crying and the man was sad and so was I. Anyway, they, they talk, and then the man, the man pretends to be her father and picks her up every Sunday and they, they take walks and see things and become very good, very good friends but other people think it's creepy that he's very good friends with a young girl and I don't want to talk about the ending because it was, it was a tragic ending and made me sad.

I don't, I don't know what it was about the movie *Sundays and Cybele*, but whatever it was I fell in love with it, I thought about it all the time, and like I said, I was fixated on it. The little girl gave an amazing performance and so did, so did the man and it just had, it just had such feeling, such, well, mother, when she finally saw it, said it had compassion and heart and it did, it had compassion and heart and beauty and mother loved it as much as I did. Father wouldn't see it because he didn't care about foreign movies with writing at the bottom of the screen.

Oh, another interesting thing was that *Sundays and Cybele* had one piece of music in it that I loved but that's not the interesting part, the interesting part is that was exactly the same as a piece of music in *The Trial*, that was the interesting part. Anyway, I wanted to, I wanted to see it again so badly, but it didn't open until February 21st in 1963 at some, some little theater in real Beverly Hills called the New Beverly Canon which was a very small little theater that didn't look so new, and I saw it fourteen times there and then, and then I followed it around wherever it played and saw it six more times. One of those times it didn't have writing on the bottom of the screen, it had English voices that, that replaced the, the real voices and that, that was disturbing because I'd, I'd gotten to know the real voices and I didn't like the fake voices at all.

Sorry to be a motormouth and yakky about *Sundays and Cybele*, but I just loved it and still love it and I did, I did see it originally at an IMPORTANT Foreign Preview. If I ever see that it's, that it's playing somewhere, which it does, then I, then I go to see it again because I, I never get tired of it.

Anyway, I was talking about that piece of music in *Sundays and Cybele* and *The Trial*. I didn't know what it was, what it was called but Nametag Walter came to the rescue and found out what it was called and it was called "Adagio in G minor" by Thomaso Albinoni and, and luckily we had one copy of it at Wallichs Music City and it must have been there for years he said, because it was a mono recording on Period Records, so I bought it and I still have it and play it all the time. I think I'll play it later before I, before I go to bed.

Anyway, now wc can, wc can move to 1963 and I can, I can see on my list for that year some great Major Studio Previews, but that wasn't the only, I mean there were, there were other things that happened that year and I guess, I guess I'll talk about some of those things, just because I'm, I'm making a record of, you know, of everything.

So, let me talk about my, let me talk about my bad car accident because that happened right at the, right at the start of the New Year and having a bad car accident was not a, not a great way to start a New Year. I was, I was on my way to mother and father's house the same way I always went, which was, which was down Olympic Boulevard and that's, that's where the bad accident happened. I was coming to Robertson and my light, my light turned green before I even got there so I, so I kept driving because the light was, the light was, you know, the light was green. And, well, all I remember is I was going through that green light when a car came through the, came through the red light and smashed right into me, I mean, into my car and the sound was horrible and I'd never, I'd never heard a sound so horrible and my car was, my car was spinning around like a, like some crazy, some crazy ride at an amusement park and, and no matter which way I turned the steering wheel it didn't matter because the car kept spinning like crazy and all I could think of was I was going to die in the spinning out-of-control car and that I'd, I'd never, I was never going to see another Major Studio Preview again because I was dead.

The car finally stopped spinning and I didn't know, I didn't know if that meant I was dead but I didn't think so because my, my heart, my heart was pounding and I was, I was shaking all over. The glass from the other side of the car, you know, the window on the door, was smashed and glass was all over the seat and I was shaking and my heart was pounding and two men were opening my door and they opened my door and got me out of the car and asked if I was okay.

I didn't know if I was okay so I didn't, I didn't know how to answer. I felt my face and, and my face was there and I, I looked at my hands and there was, there was no blood on my hands from my face, but my neck hurt and I could barely stand up. The two men said I should sit on the curb but before I could sit on the curb another man was coming up to me, and his face was red like my red sweater, not from blood but like he was mad, angry mad, and he, he screamed at me, he screamed at me that I caused the accident, that I ran a red light but I didn't because it was green but I was so shaky I couldn't even open my mouth to talk and tell him it was his fault. But I didn't have to because the two men who'd gotten me, who'd gotten me out of the car, the two men went right up to him and got really close to him and screamed back at the screaming red-faced man, telling him they saw the whole thing and that he was the one who ran the red light and he, he started to scream back and they told him to shut up and that they'd already called the police from the pay phone at the gas station and that they could smell liquor on his breath and that he, he reeked of it and was drunk.

The red-faced man screamed back and he was weaving back and forth as he screamed that he wasn't drunk but you could tell he was drunk because he looked and sounded like, like Jack Lemmon in *Days of Wine and Roses*. They told him to shut up again and he hissed at them, he hissed, I mean he hissed like a snake and then he said a bad word I won't repeat on a cassette, but it was a curse word, a bad curse word and I don't like cursing or curse words and I never cursed a bad word one time in my life and I won't start now.

Then the man tried to get back in his car like he was going to, to drive away, but the two men hauled him out of the car and held him there until the police came. The man lied to the police about who caused the bad car accident but the two men said they saw the whole thing and I told the police my light was green and the police arrested the man for being drunk and causing a bad car accident and they took him away in the police car.

I looked at my poor car, my 1953 chocolate brown Plymouth Cranbrook Belvedere, and it was, it was all smashed in on the right side, and the headlight was hanging there and the, and the whole right door was smashed and the right front tire, that was all screwy too. The two men, they were so nice and they gave me their names and phone numbers and said they'd given that to the police too. They helped me to, to walk over where the pay phone was at the gas station on the corner and I called mother and told her what, told her what had happened and she said she'd come right away and she was crying and worried but I, but I told her I thought I was okay and that the police had, had called for a tow truck and would tow it over to the gas station and we could arrange for it to be, to be taken wherever we wanted.

Mother arrived about twenty minutes later. The two men, the two men stayed with me until she got there. She looked at me and I, I must have been white as a sheet because she said look at you, you're white as a sheet. She said she'd already called the Automobile Club of America and they'd, they'd come get the car and take it to the car place that mother and father liked for car problems. Mother kept telling me I was lucky that I wasn't thrown through the windshield and decapitated. I didn't know what decapitated meant and she told me it was when your head was cut off and that didn't sound good to me. Anyway, she thanked the two men who'd helped me and I, and I thanked them too. Then she drove me to Midway Hospital and we went to, we went to the emergency room and they X-rayed my neck and said I had something called whiplash and that I'd be fine and they gave me a neck brace to, to put on my neck. When we got back to mother's, I looked in the, I looked in the mirror at me in the neck brace and I, I thought I looked like a turtle.

Anyway, I had dinner there and father said the drunk driver should be, should be welded to a jail cell. Mother dealt with the insurance companies, ours and the drunk man's. First, their insurance company said there were different stories and they said I ran the red light and they weren't going to pay. Mother knew a lawyer, the son, the son of someone she knew, and he, he, the lawyer, Marvin was his, his name, called the drunk man's insurance company and from what mother, from what mother told me, Marvin the lawyer told the insurance company we'll see you in court because there was this thing called, called a police report, that their driver was drunk, that we had two witnesses who'll come to court and testify to that and suddenly the insurance company said fine, and they made what they call a, I think it was called a settlement offer for my having to wear a neck brace for three weeks and other aches and pains.

Marvin the lawyer didn't, he didn't like the settlement offer and they went back and forth and then Marvin the lawyer accepted the settlement offer and they were, they were going to pay me $4,000 and pay the medical bills and whatever it was going to cost to fix up my car.

We put the, we put the $4,000 in the bank for a rainy day. I called Nametag Walter and told him what had happened and he said stay home for a day or two, then, then I could make up the time on the weekend. So, I went back to work after a couple of days of rest, wearing the, wearing the neck brace and, and looking like a turtle.

And that was thc, that was the way 1963 began with my, my bad car accident. I couldn't go to a Major Studio Preview for about a month because I couldn't, I couldn't sit that long in a movie theater because of my neck and, and my, my other aches and pains and because I looked like a turtle. Mother took a photo of me in my neck brace and she, and she framed it and put it on my wall and it's still there next to my signed paper from Blake Edwards and Henry Mancini.

My first Major Studio Preview in 1963 after the, after the bad car accident was at the Village in late February, an IMPORTANT Major Studio Preview. It was, it was so good to be back in a, in a movie theater and everyone at the, at the Village asked where I'd been, that there'd been a couple of Major Studio Previews I missed, and I told them about my bad car accident and the neck brace and that I, that I looked like a turtle and they were all, they were all very nice and said they were glad I was in one piece because they didn't like it when Preview Harvey wasn't there for a preview, that I was like, that I was like, like family.

The IMPORTANT Major Studio Preview was called *The Courtship of Eddie's Father*, starring Glenn Ford from *Experiment in Terror* and I enjoyed it, and it was better than good good and had funny parts. It was in drab Metrocolor and while the movie screen was wide, this one wasn't called Cinemascope it was, it was called something new, it was called Panavision. I didn't, I didn't see much difference between Panavision and Cinemascope and I, and I liked the name Cinemascope better than the name Panavision. Anyway, I liked the movie and it was better than good good, oh, and the, and the manager of the Village introduced me to a man from M-G-M who was happy to hear I liked the movie. He told me the Paramount man had told him about me and that he should, that he should meet me, Preview Harvey.

Oh, and I forgot, I forgot about the Academy Award nominations and then the Academy Awards. The, the nominations were announced right before I saw *The Courtship of Eddie's Father*. They were, they were announced on February 25th and I was, I was hoping that some of the Major Studio Previews I'd loved would be, would be up for Academy Awards, you know, nominated.

Anyway, they were listed, the nominations were listed in the, in the newspaper and I found the nominations very interesting. Like the director of the small picture *David and Lisa* was nominated but Blake Edwards wasn't and he was my favorite and I was sad that he, that he wasn't nominated. But Jack Lemmon was up for best, for best actor and Lee Remick was up for best actress for, for *Days of Wine and Roses* and I was, I was rooting for them to win. *Experiment in Terror* didn't get nominated for anything. *Days of Wine and Roses* got other nominations too, like Art Direction, Black-and-White and Costume Design, Black-and-White, and Henry Mancini was nominated for Best Song for *Days of Wine and Roses*. Oh yeah, I can't forget the most important, the most important thing, *Sundays and Cybele* was nominated for, for Best Foreign Film. Anyway, the ceremony wasn't until April, so I, so I just, I just had to wait to see if what I was rooting for would win.

I saw three more Major Studio Previews that weren't even good good so I don't, I don't really want to even talk about them because why? Okay, okay, I'll say what they were but won't talk about them. One was called *Papa's Delicate Condition* with Jackie Gleason, that one was, well, oh wait, I'm not talking about it, the second one was called *Call Me Bwana* with Bob Hope and then the third one was called *My Six Loves* with Debbie Reynolds. They were all stinkers and the other preview nuts thought they were too. Luckily, there were somc good ones waiting, waiting around the corner, but first the Academy Awards happened. I went to mother and father's to watch it because I didn't, I didn't have a TV, so I went there and we all watched it except father kept falling asleep and then he'd, then he'd wake up and say who won then he'd, then he'd fall back asleep before we could even tell him. Mother said to me your father has become a narcoleptic. I didn't know that meant so she told me it meant someone who has the tendency to fall asleep at the drop of a hat wherever they are. I asked her where she learned, where she learned words like that and she said *Ben Casey.*

Anyway, I was rooting for *Days of Wine and Roses* and *Sundays and Cybele. Days of Wine and Roses* lost in all their categories but finally it won, it won for Best Song, so that was good and we all cheered, well mother and I, mother and I cheered because father was busy being a narcoleptic. And then *Sundays and Cybele* won for Best Foreign Film and mother and I cheered for that and our cheering, our cheering woke up father who said who won? It was, it was a fun night and the two movies I was, that I was rooting for each won an award.

The next night I saw another Major Studio Preview and another stinker, *The Man from the Diners' Club* with Danny Kaye, directed by my favorite, Frank Tashlin. I loved Danny Kaye and I loved Frank Tashlin but *The Man from the Diners' Club* didn't, it didn't, it didn't get a single laugh for the entire movie. It was a Columbia picture and I, I thanked my lucky stars that I, that I didn't know anyone from Columbia. I was wondering when I'd see a good Major Studio Preview again and I finally saw one I liked at the Picwood called *The List of Adrian Messenger,* that one was fun and had good actors, George C. Scott and a bunch, and a bunch of guest stars like Tony Curtis and Frank Sinatra and Robert Mitchum and Burt Lancaster and, and Kirk Douglas, but you didn't know it was them because they were in disguises and made up to not look like them, then after the mystery had been solved, then, then they all came on screen at the end and took off their makeup. I'd never seen that in a movie before. Anyway, I liked it. I was, I was now seeing as many Major Studio Previews at the Picwood as I was at the Village.

The next Major Studio Preview was at the Village and it was a Jerry Lewis picture and it was, it was even funnier than *The Bellboy*, and the audience, the audience roared with laughter and it was called *The Nutty Professor* and it was in Technicolor and the Technicolor color was, was amazing. I loved it and couldn't wait, couldn't wait to see it again. After the movie, I was outside and one of the ushers told me that Jerry Lewis was there and pointed me to where he was, which was at the very end of the, the very end of the lobby. So, I walked over there and stood there hoping he'd see me and he, he did see me and he said wait a minute, I remember you and that baseball cap, don't tell me, don't tell me. Preview Harvey! I said that's me and I reminded him that he gave me that name and he said I know I gave you that name am I senile? Then he made some Jerry Lewis noises that made me laugh really loud like I had during the, during the movie.

Then he said, well don't just stand there like a plant that died, what did you think? These people I'm with want to know what you thought because all they do is worry about money. I was still laughing at the plant that died and he said in his Jerry Lewis voice as loud as he could Preeeeeeviewwww Harveeeeeyyyyy did you like the picture, tell us, you can't keep Jews waiting, they get a hernia. I managed to, to stop laughing and I told him I loved it and laughed my head off and he said did you find your head and put it back on and I started laughing all over again. Then he said to the people he was with Preview Harvey loved it and the last time I saw him he loved *The Bellboy* and said it was gonna be a hit and it was a hit and so now maybe this one will be a hit too. I said oh it will be and I told him I'd just seen three Major Studio Preview stinkers in a row. Jerry Lewis suddenly, out of the blue, kissed the top of my Hollywood Stars baseball cap and said I love this guy. I told mother all about it and she said you're becoming a regular celebrity.

I wasn't, I wasn't, you know, I wasn't a regular celebrity because a regular celebrity didn't work at Wallichs Music City and bring Swiss cheese with mustard sandwiches on Weber's Bread to work in a paper bag. A regular celebrity would be eating at the, at the Brown Derby up the street. People like, people like me, just people, didn't eat at the Brown Derby although I had $4,000 in the bank and could have if I wanted to but they probably wouldn't, they probably wouldn't let me wear my Hollywood Stars baseball cap because it was a ritzy place. There was a, a coffee shop I liked called Coffee Dan's and I ate there once every few weeks, just for a, for a change of pace. I liked their food and it wasn't too expensive and I, I, I didn't even have to dip into my $4,000, which I was, which I was saving for a rainy day.

Oh, I forgot, I forgot to say that my car was, my car was all better and like new when I got it back from the repair people and so that was good.

Anyway, I saw more Major Studio Previews and they got, they got better and better with only a few stinkers. Some Major Studio Previews I really liked were, well, let me, let me start with the best one, I saw it at the Paramount and it was, it was called *The Great Escape* and it was about people in a, I think they called it a prisoner camp or a prisoner war camp or something like that and all they wanted to do was escape and they dug three tunnels and tried to, tried to escape but the guards found out and stopped it and shot one of the prisoners who tried to go over a wall but they kept working on the tunnels and finally a lot of them escaped but some were killed and only three got away and it was, it was exciting and funny and the actors were great, all of them, and the music was exciting and the best, the best scene of all was a motorcycle chase, that was the best scene. The most amazing part was that the movie, the movie was almost three hours long but it didn't, it didn't seem almost three hours long at all and I loved it. It was an M-G-M picture in Panavision and color and the, and the M-G-M man I met at *The Courtship of Eddie's Father* was there and asked what I thought and I told him it was amazing and I thought it would be a big, a very big hit and he told me he was really glad to hear it because everyone was, everyone at M-G-M was worried about the long running time because that meant less showings a day, but I told him that it didn't, it didn't seem long and I still thought it would be a big hit.

At the Picwood, I saw a Major Studio Preview in Panavision and black-and-white. Even before the title came on the screen, a blonde woman walked out of a door and I could, I could see immediately that it was Yvette Mimieux so I had to like it whatever it was because she was so beautiful and sensitive. The Major Studio Preview was called *Toys in the Attic* and Dean Martin was the star and it was very dramatic and there was one scene, well, there was one scene where I had to, where I had to look away because, because someone got their, got their throat cut and I couldn't, I couldn't look at that because that was disturbing. I thought it was a weird movie and the weirdest part was that one of the sisters in the movie seemed to, seemed to, well, one of the sisters in the movie seemed to like her brother too much, I mean, in the wrong way, and that's what, that's what leads to the tragedy. Tragedy, that's a good word for movies like *Toys in the Attic* and even though it was very dramatic and a little weird I liked it.

The most interesting Major Studio Preview was at the, was at the Bruin across from the Village. The Major Studio Preview was called *The Caretakers*, with Joan Crawford and a lot of women with mental problems or conditions. But that wasn't, that wasn't the interesting part. The interesting part was right at the beginning of the movie when a woman is buying a ticket to see a movie and the movie theater she's going to is the, is the Bruin, the same movie theater we were in seeing *The Caretakers*. She went in the lobby and, and, and that was the lobby we'd all just been in. Then she goes into the theater and it was the same theater we were all sitting in watching *The Caretakers* and then she suddenly had mental problems and she was screaming and going crazy in front of the movie screen, the same movie screen we were watching and she screams some more and then they take her away to a mental institution but we were still in the theater watching *The Caretakers*.

That was weird, being in the movie theater that was in the movie we were watching, that was just weird. I liked the movie and the patients were all, they all had mental problems and, and after seeing the movie I knew that I never wanted to go to a, to a mental institution or be put in a, in a strait-jacket. Joan Crawford had very nice clothes for a head lady nurse who worked in a mental institution with straitjackets and, and padded cells. She always looked like she was, like she was going to a cocktail party. I liked the music especially the exciting, the exciting music during the titles. We got the album in at Wallichs Music City and I bought it and played it a lot, especially the exciting music from the titles. Every time I played that album I thanked my lucky stars I wasn't in a straitjacket or padded cell or, or mental institution with a, with a nurse in nice clothes like Joan Crawford.

Oh, Nate and Joe and Gary and I met another preview nut. He came over and said hello and said that he'd seen us at all the previews and that we always, we always talked and he was, he said he was too shy to come over but finally after all this time he did come over and we all thought he was very nice and he'd been going to previews since he was twelve when he and his family moved here from some place, from some place called Solana Beach. His name was Terrence and he loved Major Studio Previews and wanted to know if he could, if he could, you know, talk with us before and after previews and of course that was fine with us. Terrence was a Negro and wore glasses, and he was, he always wore very nice clothes and he was, he was smart and he became part of our group.

Anyway, there were a couple of other preview nuts that we noticed but they never joined our group, although they might, they might wave or smile or something and I, I don't think that they were as fixated on previews as we were but I didn't know that for a, for a fact because, because we never talked to them.

In the last part of the summer, I didn't go to as many Major Studio Previews because Nametag Walter asked if I could work extra on the weekends and some evenings and I, I said I could and I made more money when I worked extra on the weekends so that was nice. The store was very crowded all the time in the summer because of the young people and their, and their rock-and-roll records.

We sold lots of 45s and the, the big sellers that I liked were "End of the World," "Rhythm of the Rain" because I loved rain, "Blue Velvet," and "Puff, the Magic Dragon." The Henry Mancini 45 of "Days and Wine and Roses" sold very well, but not as well as the, as the Andy Williams version, and I loved that one too because, because Andy Williams had such a smooth voice. Oh, and here's the interesting thing about the Andy Williams 45. The other side of the 45 was a song I liked called "Can't Get Used to Losing You" and people asked for that one as much as they did for "Days of Wine and Roses," even though they were both on the same record and it was like, it was like you got two hits for the, for the price of one.

I also liked a song that didn't have words, it just had music and it was called "Our Winter Love," and I, I liked it because it was, it was like pretty movie music, and another song I liked was, was called "Go Away, Little Girl," by Steve Lawrence, another singer with a smooth voice. Mother told me I was, she said I was tone deaf when I tried to sing along with a song. I thought deaf was when you couldn't hear, but she said tone deaf was when you couldn't sing along because what you were singing wasn't what the other person was singing, that's what, that's what tone deaf meant. But since I was tone deaf that meant that I couldn't tell that I was tone deaf so I could sing along and it didn't matter if I was tone deaf or not.

I saw a Major Studio Preview at the Crest in Westwood, called *Lilies of the Field* about Sidney Poitier and nuns and it was a very good movie and I liked Sidney Poitier because he seemed like a nice person especially with nuns.

At the Village I saw a Major Studio Preview called *Under the Yum Yum Tree* with Jack Lemmon and some pretty girls but no one laughed very much and I, I didn't think it was going to be a hit because no one laughed very much, including me and I didn't think Jack Lemmon would be, you know, would be nominated for an Academy Award for *Under the Yum Yum Tree* like he was for *Days of Wine and Roses.*

I saw another Major Studio Preview comedy at the Paramount called *Mary, Mary* starring Debbie Reynolds, about a woman named Mary but I thought there'd be two Marys since the title said Mary twice, but there was only one Mary and the movie was okay good not good good but it had some parts where we all laughed. I also saw a Studio Preview called *Lord of the Flies* at the new luxurious Lido Theater and that was a very strange movie but I really liked it because it was strange and disturbing about a group of boys, schoolboys, on an island with no, with no adults and some of the boys become very mean, especially to a chubby boy named Piggy, and the bad boys do bad things until adults finally arrive at the end. I knew about bad boys doing bad things because they did that to me in school, the bad boys did all that stuff to me in school and so I knew how that, I knew how that felt. None of the preview nuts were there because I guess they liked the bigger theaters not the new luxurious Lido kind of theater but I liked seeing smaller strange movies too, so I was fine with the new luxurious Lido Theater.

Then in October I saw a few Major Studio Previews that I loved. The first Major Studio Preview I saw, well, it wasn't a Major Studio Preview it was a Sneak Preview and I almost didn't, I almost didn't go because it wasn't a Major Studio Preview, but I'm glad I took a chance because I liked the movie so much and it was, it was interesting and surprising in a few ways that I'll talk about. I saw it at the Criterion Theater, a nice theater in, in Santa Monica. The Sneak Preview was another black-and-white movie and it was called *Soldier in the Rain* and I liked it right away because I liked anything with rain. It was with Jackie Gleason and Steve McQueen and I loved Steve McQueen from *The Great Escape* so that was exciting and then it said A Blake Edwards Production and I was, I was confused because this wasn't previewing at the Village where I'd seen the other Blake Edwards previews, and then why wasn't it a Major Studio rather than Allied Artists, that was confusing too. The music that played while the titles were on was fun and I knew immediately it was my, my favorite, Henry Mancini, because there was no mistaking his, there was no mistaking his music. So, I already knew I loved it and then it said Tuesday Weld and I couldn't wait, couldn't wait for it to start because I loved Tuesday Weld. It said the screenplay was by Maurice Richlin and Blake Edwards, but then, but then the big surprising thing was that it didn't, it didn't say Directed by Blake Edwards like all his movies did, it said Directed by Ralph Nelson and I remembered that name because, because he directed the movie I saw a few weeks before, *Lilies of the Field.* I wondered why Blake Edwards didn't direct *Soldier in the Rain* and I wondered, I wondered if he was at the Sneak Preview.

Anyway, I really enjoyed the movie and some of it was funny and some of it was not sad but, but, kind of, kind of melancholy, I think that's the word. There was beautiful music that was, it was, well, it was just like the rain, the kind of, the kind of music you'd listen to in the rain or watching the rain from your window. Tuesday Weld was even more adorable than before and I, I wanted to marry her all over again. Oh, and Mr. Edwards wasn't at the Sneak Preview so I couldn't, you know, I couldn't, I couldn't ask him why he didn't direct *Soldier in the Rain.*

After that, I, I hit a bonanza of Major Studio Previews that I loved, one after another. All of the preview nuts, we all felt the same way about this whole batch. First there was a Major Studio Preview at the Wilshire Theater and the ad in the newspaper for the Major Studio Preview at the Wilshire didn't just say Major Studio Preview it said Tonight at 8:30 The Fox Wilshire Theatre proudly presents an important Major Studio Preview Technicolor with TWO GREAT STARS! I'd, I'd never seen that in an ad before so I, I was, well, I couldn't wait for work to be done.

As soon as I got off work I drove to the Wilshire and got my good seat because I, I figured it would be jam-packed from an ad like that. They were playing a movie called *A New Kind of Love* with Paul Newman and Joanne Woodward and it was, it was not even good good or okay good, it was a stinker.

At 8:00 there was an intermission and I looked around and of course I saw the preview nuts including the ones we didn't know but who waved at us. Nate and Joe and Gary and Terrence came over to where I was and they, they also said that they'd, they'd never seen an ad quite like that one and were excited to see what the Major Studio Preview was going to be. Nate's condition seemed to be, to be worse than usual, with the constant jerky movements and, and shudders, and some people were looking at him when it happened because I guess they'd never seen anything like that before. Oh, and Joe had a new suit and it looked just like his old suit except it was blue instead of brown.

Anyway, they went and got their seats and the theater was completely full and the lights went down and the movie started and it was A Universal Picture and then there was a train and a body fell off the train or maybe it was thrown off the train and the body rolled down a hill and was dead, so I already liked it. Then music started and there were colorful arrows all over the screen, like cartoon arrows going this way and that way and making spirals and then those turned into moving wavy colorful lines and it said Cary Grant and Audrey Hepburn and the audience applauded really loud because they were TWO GREAT STARS and there was excited chatter while the title of the movie came on, *Charade*. Then the rest of the titles played while the exciting music played and I knew the exciting music had to be Henry Mancini again because it just sounded like Henry Mancini and then it said Music by Henry Mancini so I was right. It seemed like Mr. Mancini wrote music for a lot of movies.

So, the ad was right about TWO GREAT STARS, Cary Grant and Audrey Hepburn and I'll, I'll just say that everyone loved it and it was just so, so, it was just so clever and funny and suspenseful and had surprising surprises especially at the end. The TWO GREAT STARS were great and Audrey Hepburn looked even more beautiful than in, than in *Breakfast at*

Tiffany's, and I, I didn't know how that was, how that was even possible and Cary Grant was, he was, Cary Grant was so suave and debonair and handsome and you didn't know if he was the good guy or the bad guy and it kept, it kept everyone guessing right up to the end. All the preview nuts agreed that it was going to be a, it was going to be a big hit.

The next Major Studio Preview was back at the, at the Paramount and it was another one I, that I loved. Well, before I talk about it I have to change cassette tapes again so I don't run out in the, in the middle of, you know, in the middle of, of talking.

CASSETTE SIX

Okay, the cassette ran out of, ran out of tape, so now a new cassette is in and now I can, now I can talk about the preview at the Paramount. We were all there, all us, all us preview nuts and we were, we were talking about how Major Studio Previews at the end of the year, like in November, meant you might see one of the, one of the big Christmas pictures so we all hoped that that's what we were, that we were going to get.

So, it was an M-G-M picture and there was exciting music when the lion was roaring, and then it said it took place in Stockholm and I didn't know where that was but, but then we found out it was in Sweden and it was about the Nobel Prize and who was winning the prize. Paul Newman and Edward G. Robinson were the stars and I, and I liked Edward G. Robinson because he was, he was short like me, and the movie was called *The Prize* and it was a very colorful story with some intrigue, funny things, villains, and a pretty blonde lady and it got a, it got a great reaction from the audience especially the scene where Paul Newman is trying to escape from the villains and ends up in a, a, a place where everyone is naked and he tries wearing a towel but they don't allow towels and it was really funny but you never really saw anyone naked so that was good because I don't really want to see a bunch of naked people naked, I don't even like to see me naked but that was a funny scene. There's a happy ending where everything works out for everyone and it was just such a fun picture and the kind that you could see a few times, which I, which I did when it opened at the Stanley Warner Beverly Hills.

After it was over, we were, we were in the lobby, which is very lush and big. Anyway, we were, we were talking about how much we liked the movie and the M-G-M man was there and he was, he was kind of walking around listening to people's comments and he saw me and he, he came over and said how did you like the movie and I said I thought it was a really fun picture and that I thought it was going to be a big hit because the audience had such a good time and he said he was glad to hear it and that I'd been right about *The Great Escape* being a big hit and he, he wished me a happy holiday season.

Then something very bad happened, not to me, a bad thing didn't happen to me but a bad thing happened to everyone, just a week after the preview of *The Prize*. I was at work at Wallichs Music City on a Friday, doing my, you know, doing my usual sorting and filing and making listening copies and all that and Nametag Walter came in the back room where I was and he looked like I looked after my bad car accident, white as a sheet. I didn't know if I should, if I should, you know, if I should say anything, but Nametag Walter was white as a sheet and had tears in his eyes. I still didn't know if I should say anything to him or not but before I could, before I could decide whether to say something or not, he said something to me. He said have you heard the news? I said no because I was in the back making listening copies of the latest album releases and he said it's terrible, just terrible and I said what's terrible and he said and he could barely get the words to come out, he said someone shot President Kennedy, he's dead.

I knew who President Kennedy was because who didn't know who President Kennedy was and I knew it was, I knew it was a very bad thing that President Kennedy had been shot and was dead and all I could think of to say to Nametag Walter was I'm sorry and all he could say back was what kind of world is this? He said we were, that we were going to close early in thirty minutes and so I could just go home and I, I didn't want to go home but he looked, he looked sad so I got my coat and went out into the store. People were, people were there, gathered around where the TV sets and record players were sold, watching the news, most of them, most of them crying. I didn't want to watch because, because everyone was so sad and crying but I heard some of what they were saying about how it had, how it had happened. Anyway, I left and drove right to mother and father's for our Friday night dinner.

When she opened the door I could, I could see that mother had been crying and she said did you hear the terrible news and I said yes and that Nametag Walter had been white as a sheet and crying and that, and that he'd said what kind of world is this. She told me that stores and movie theaters were closing because of what happened and she hoped I wasn't planning on seeing a Major Studio Preview. I wasn't because there was, there was only one that night and it was in Inglewood and I didn't, I didn't like the sound of Inglewood and didn't want to go there even for a Major Studio Preview.

Mother made franks and beans because that was one of, that was one of father's favorite things to eat and we sat down at the table and he said to mother can we turn the TV off while we eat, can we do that? They just say the same things over and over again and I've heard it for three hours now and I'd like to eat in peace. Mother got up and turned the TV off and said we're turning it on after dessert and father said fine you do that.

We ate the franks and beans and they were good but no one really said anything, which was, which was unusual because we always were yakky at dinner. After dessert, which was peach pie a la mode, father went and sat down on the sofa and turned on the TV and flipped through all the, he flipped through all the channels trying to find something to watch, but every channel was still talking about President Kennedy being killed and what the, what the latest details were.

Anyway, he immediately fell asleep so it, it didn't matter what they were talking about. I helped mother with the, with the dishes, and she was sad and said everyone in the country was sad and I thought I should be sad but I didn't like to be sad even though I knew that President Kennedy being killed was a, a, you know, a sad thing. I went home at nine and since I didn't have a TV I didn't have to watch all the stations talk about President Kennedy being killed.

The next day, the next day it was in all the, in all the newspapers and everybody was still sad and there were no Major Studio Previews and I didn't even know if the movie theaters were, were, you know, I didn't know if they were open. But for the rest of the month there wasn't even one Major Studio Preview or any kind of preview and I could, I could never remember that happening before, not since I became fixated on previews. It was probably because everyone was still sad and didn't want to, didn't want to go to the movies at all, but after more than a week of sad it was December and I, and I was ready to see more Major Studio Previews. Unfortunately, there weren't many because, well, I don't know why, other than maybe they didn't, maybe they didn't think anyone would come.

But I did see two Major Studio Previews and, and interestingly they were at the same theater and only three days apart, one on a Wednesday and one on a Saturday. The theater was the Stanley Warner Beverly Hills on Wilshire and the Wednesday one was an IMPORTANT Major Studio Preview in Color. The thing I couldn't understand was that the movie playing there was called *Wuthering Heights* and when I, when I told mother about it, she said that was an old movie from 1939 and I, I wasn't even, I wasn't even born yet so why were they showing a movie from 1939?

Anyway, I got there about thirty minutes before the preview and I was surprised to see that the, that the theater only had about fifty people in it and I'd never seen that before at a Major Studio Preview or any preview. Anyway, it was a movie called *Kings of the Sun* with Yul Brynner and, and the guy from *West Side Story*, George Chakiris. I didn't even know what to, what to say about it because, because I didn't understand a word anyone was saying or what the story was or where they were or what they, what was going on. By the end of the movie there were only about twenty of us left. None of the other preview nuts were there and it was, it was maybe the biggest stinker I'd ever seen and I'd seen some big stinkers.

The Saturday preview was an IMPORTANT Studio Preview and the ad said A Delightful Comedy. It was an American-International movie, I guess that was the studio and it was called *The Comedy of Terrors* and it had a lot of, a lot of scary actors in it like Peter Lorre and Vincent Price and Boris Karloff and Basil Rathbone. I'm not sure why it was IMPORTANT and I didn't think it was a, a delightful comedy although the actors were all trying to act funny and the music was so annoying because it was trying to be funny and there were a few times I laughed but I didn't really care for it and I had to say it was another stinker. Maybe they didn't want to preview anything good until people weren't, until people weren't sad anymore.

But I saved the one good IMPORTANT Preview I saw for last because it was, it was a very powerful story and another small movie. It was at the new luxurious Lido and the double bill playing there was *The L-Shaped Room* and my, my favorite, *Sundays and Cybele*, so I made sure I got there in time to see that first and I, and I loved it as much as ever. The IMPORTANT Preview was called *Ladybug Ladybug* and I didn't know any of the actors in it but I, I recognized the name of the director, Frank Perry, because he directed *David and Lisa*, and I liked that movie very much.

Anyway, it was a very powerful story about an alert going off at a school, you know, one of those, one of those nuclear bomb alerts and all the kids are sent home. One of the kids lives in a house that has a, that has a bomb shelter and they go in there. One girl who went home, her parents weren't there and she, she goes to the bomb shelter house but they won't let her in because there's not enough room and she panics and hides in an, in an old refrigerator that's been left somewhere. Then one of the nice boys leaves the bomb shelter to find her but he hears a loud noise and thinks it's the, that it's the end of the world and keeps yelling STOP, STOP, STOP! I thought it was a really good small movie and that was the last preview I saw in 1963.

So, so then came 1964 and there were some really great Major Studio Previews in 1964 and I'll just, I'll just tell you about the great ones and, and maybe I'll mention a few stinkers, but mostly I saw wonderful Major Studio Previews in 1964 and it started with the very first one I saw in January and, and 1964 couldn't have, couldn't have started off better and not only that, not only that but the first preview I saw solved a mystery too, I mean, well not a mystery but something I was confused about, so it solved a confusion.

The movie playing at the Village was *Love with the Proper Stranger* and I really wanted to, to see that one because Steve McQueen and Natalie Wood were the stars and I, they were two of my favorites and I wanted to marry Natalie Wood because of *West Side Story*, so I got there early so I could see that one. Everyone at the Village said hi to me and the candy counter girl already had my Dots out as soon as she saw me and that's, that's why I loved going to the Village most of all, even though other theaters knew me but not like the Village. I got my good seat and watched *Love with the Proper Stranger*, and I really thought it was great and I loved Steve McQueen and Natalie Wood and the song in the movie, sung by Jack Jones and of course I, I bought the 45 the next day at Wallichs Music City.

Anyway, after the movie all us preview nuts were there so I talked to our group and they all said what they'd done for the holidays, which was nothing, and I said what I'd done, which was nothing but working and going to mother and father's on Christmas Day, and then we all took our seats so we could watch the Major Studio Preview.

The beginning of the movie was a scene so we didn't know what it was or who was in it, which was, which was kind of fun for a change. Anyway, a young girl princess is given the biggest diamond in the world by her father and it's, it's the most unusual too because if you, if you look closely into the diamond you can see something that resembles a leaping panther and the diamond is called the Pink Panther.

Then we see into the diamond and that's when the, when the titles finally started and it was a, it was a cartoon, a cartoon with a Pink Panther and it was so clever and the movie was called *The Pink Panther* and I knew I loved it because it said A Blake Edwards Production. I knew some of the cast and recognized Peter Sellers' name because he was in *Road to Hong Kong* and was funny. Oh, and the, and the music that played over the titles was really fun and catchy and clever and I knew it was Henry Mancini because, because who else could it be in a Blake Edwards movie? I was right about that and then, and then it said Directed by Blake Edwards and I thought maybe that, maybe that solved my confusion of why someone else directed that movie *Soldier in the Rain* because Blake Edwards was probably directing this movie when that movie was made.

Anyway, it was the best movie, so funny and I loved all the actors, especially Peter Sellers, who was, who was so funny as a bumbling French detective named Inspector Clouseau. His first scene in the, in the movie got the biggest laugh that I'd ever heard in a movie and you couldn't even, you couldn't even hear the next scene because the laugh was so long and so loud. But every scene he was in got big long loud laughs like you've never heard. The grown-up princess was played by a lady named Claudia Cardinale and, and, and she was, well, she was so beautiful and of course I wanted to marry her. At the end of the movie, the audience clapped and clapped.

I know, I know I'm like a, I'm like a broken record, but after the movie I saw Mr. Edwards who was there with another group of people. The difference, the difference was that this time the manager found me and said Mr. Edwards was hoping I'd be here and he took me over to the group and Mr. Edwards and Mr. Edwards looked at me and said there he is, my good luck charm. I said hello, Mr. Edwards and he said well, let's have it and I said it was the funniest thing I'd ever seen and I laughed so hard that I, that I couldn't catch my breath and that I loved Inspector Clouseau and that I could see a whole movie with just him and Mr. Edwards smiled at me with a, with a gleam in his eye. Then he turned to his group and said folks we have the Preview Harvey seal of approval and my good luck charm hasn't been wrong yet. He thanked me for being there and for being such a good luck charm and asked if I ever took my Hollywood Stars baseball cap off and I told him only when I sleep and that made him laugh.

I told mother all about it and she couldn't, she couldn't wait to see it and I told her how nice it was to hear people laughing so hard after all the, the President Kennedy sadness. She said something I've said a million zillion times since, she said laughter is good for what ails you. The movie didn't come out until March 20th and mother, father, and I all went to the 6:30 show the day it opened exclusively at the, at the Paramount. Of course, I bought the album the day we got it in at Wallichs Music City. I didn't really see how any Major Studio Preview was going to top *The Pink Panther* that year.

A week later I went to a Major Studio Preview at the Wilshire. The movie playing there, *The Victors*, wasn't for me because, because it was a, it was a war picture and I didn't like war pictures. I got there in time for the Major Studio Preview and got a good seat, and, you know, it wasn't hard to, to get a good seat when you were, when you just needed one seat. The theater was full and of course the preview nuts were there and we all were yakky for a while. Anyway, anyway the preview started and there was writing that said something about the events in the movie couldn't really happen because there were safeguards to prevent that and that nothing in the movie was based on real events or people.

Then there was a mountain with fog all around it and a, and a narrator said something about rumors of the Russians and a doomsday machine and I didn't know what any of that meant but I was, I was hoping it wasn't a war movie. Then the titles came on and there was really romantic music playing, like when a kissing scene would be happening only it wasn't a, it wasn't a kissing scene it was two airplanes, one with a long thing coming out of it that attached to the plane below it. I think they were, I think it was some kind of refueling thing, but the romantic kissing music caused everyone to laugh really loud and I laughed too, even though I didn't know why it was funny.

The first name on the screen was, and I couldn't, I couldn't believe it, it was Peter Sellers so I knew we were in for a funny movie because he was so funny in *The Pink Panther.* I didn't recognize the other actor names. The title of the movie was the longest title I'd ever seen in a movie, *Dr. Strangelove or: How I Learned to Stop Worrying and Love the Bomb.* Anyway, it was the weirdest movie because sometimes it seemed like it was really serious and most of the time people were, people were screaming with laughter, me included.

Everything in the movie seemed like it could really happen despite the writing at the beginning of the movie. It took me a little while to, to figure out that Peter Sellers was playing three different roles, he played three different roles and each role was completely different and he looked and sounded different in each role and he was, he was beyond amazing but so funny in all three roles but especially the President of the United States and also *Dr. Strangelove* and I don't know how he did that, I just don't. But everyone was great in it and it actually got some bigger laughs than *The Pink Panther* and it was scary and funny at the same time and it was another movie that was, that was like nothing else I'd ever seen. Us preview nuts loved it and I was curious to see if it would be a hit.

It opened about a month later and for the first time, for the first time I read some reviews because I was, I was so curious to see if they liked it or not. I kind of got fixated on reading reviews after that and I actually went to mother's and opened the magazines on the coffee table to read *Time* and *Newsweek* and *Saturday Review* and I read the ones in the newspapers or I read the ads for the movies where they used review quotes in the ads.

Anyway, the first review I read was in the *Los Angeles Times* by someone named Philip K. Scheuer and he hated the movie so much it was, it was actually shocking how much he hated the movie. I cut it out of the newspaper because it was so shocking that I wanted to, I wanted to save it. I also cut out the ad with quotes in it so I'd, I'd have that, and with the magazines on the coffee table I wrote down parts of them so I'd have them because mother wouldn't let me cut anything out of her coffee table magazines.

So, the Philip K. Scheuer review said, "After suffering through two screenings of *Dr. Strangelove*, I would sooner drink hemlock." I, I had to look up what hemlock is and it's, it's poison. Then he wrote, "To me, *Dr. Strangelove* is an evil thing" and he went on and on and on about how much he hated the movie and I thought he was full of franks and beans because I, I loved the movie. The review quotes used in the ad were, well, they said exactly what I felt. I pulled out the ad so I could say the quotes on here, on the cassette, just to have a record of it. *Life* said, "*Dr. Strangelove* is a wildly comic nightmare!" *Newsweek* said, "Crazy, fantastic, outrageous and side-splittingly funny!" and, and that's what I thought but they wrote it better than I could say it. *New Yorker* said, "The Best American Movie in Years!" and *Esquire* said: "A laf-forama! The funniest and most serious American movie in a long time!"

So, from then on, I liked to read reviews for movies, to see if anyone felt exactly like I did and sometimes they did and sometimes they didn't and I, I started cutting out the reviews and saving them. Oh, and sometimes they had interesting information in them, like one review I read of *Dr. Strangelove* said that it was, that it was supposed to come out in late November of 1963 but was cancelled because of President Kennedy and they said there were other movies that were cancelled too because they had presidents in them like *Seven Days in May*, *Kisses for My President*, and *Fail Safe*, they'd all been postponed and would be coming out during the year now that time had passed and that was, that was interesting.

So, here are some of the, some of the other Major Studio Previews I liked in 1964. I'll, I'll try not to be too yakky about them because that's all I've been, that's all I've been doing on all these cassette tapes so maybe I'll be a little, maybe I'll be a little not so yakky from now on but sometimes I don't, I don't, I'm not aware that I'm being so yakky and I have no off button.

One of my favorites I saw at the Village in Cinemascope and black-and-white was called *The Third Secret* and I didn't know the actors at all, well, maybe I'd seen them in something because they looked familiar, but I, I didn't know their names. It took place in England and an analyst has killed himself and that's the official report but his, his young daughter doesn't believe it and thinks one of her father's patients killed him and there are four patients and a TV reporter is one of them and, and he maybe thinks he did it but goes to the other patients and it's, it's all very mysterious until there's a surprise ending and we find out what the third secret is because the daughter told the reporter there were three secrets, the ones we don't tell people, the ones we don't tell ourselves and the third secret is a secret but at the end, at the end she says the third secret is the truth but he's already found out the truth that the daughter was one of her father's patients and she killed him because she, she's got mental problems and thought he was, he was going to put her away in a mental institution and she suddenly stabs the reporter but he lives and she's put away and he visits her and says he'll keep visiting and that was the end. The young girl who played the young girl was wonderful and her name was Pamela Franklin and after the movie, I, I wrote down the three secrets in the car just to remember them.

So, here are some, here are some others I enjoyed at Major Studio Previews but I don't want to be too yakky about. A movie called *Girl with Green Eyes*, and the lead actress Rita Tushingham had the biggest eyes I'd ever seen anywhere, but the funny part, not funny funny, but the funny part was how could we know her eyes were green when the movie was in black-and-white? Anyway, I liked Rita Tushingham and her big eyes, they were like those, those paintings with big eyes that mother liked.

Oh, one thing I haven't talked about yet and it's not about Major Studio Previews but maybe I'll just, I'll just talk about it because I'm, I'm making a record of things and one thing I haven't talked about yet that just, that just popped into my head is how many celebrities came into Wallichs Music City and sometimes, sometimes when I was filing records or putting new listening copies out I'd see them. I saw Johnny Mathis there once and I liked his voice because it was smooth, but the biggest celebrities I saw were, were Burt Lancaster and Rock Hudson and Red Skelton, who mother loved from his TV shows. I never talked to any of them but it was, it was fun to see them or stand near them and they all seemed like very nice people. Oh wait, I forgot that I did, I did talk to Johnny Mathis because he asked me where he could find a record he was looking for and I took him to where it was and he thanked me for being so helpful and I told him I enjoyed his records and that he had a smooth voice and he said that was very sweet of me to say, so I did talk to Johnny Mathis. Anyway, I just wanted to mention that on a cassette because, because it happened.

Okay, so I did see a couple of stinkers and I'll just say their names but I won't, I won't be yakky about them, but the couple of stinkers were *Honeymoon Hotel*, that was a stinker, and *Woman of Straw* starring a woman whose name I couldn't figure out when it came on the screen and I can't even pronounce it now probably, Gina Lolo, Gina Lolobridgesomething, Lolobridgeta, something like that, I don't know but the movie was a stinker because it was too confusing and I didn't understand the story or anything and it was, it was weird seeing the actor Sean Connery in it because he wasn't James Bond and I'd seen him in that James Bond movie *From Russia With Love* where he was James Bond and that was a good movie that was playing with one of my Major Studio Previews when it, when it came out.

Anyway, here are more Major Studio Previews I saw. At the Paramount, I saw *The Unsinkable Molly Brown* with Debbie Reynolds and she was, she was very energetic and loud and it was a, it was a musical movie and had songs and dancing and I enjoyed it and it was an M-G-M picture and the M-G-M man was there and I told him I enjoyed it very much and that I thought it would be a hit.

Then I saw an IMPORTANT Major Studio Preview at that theater in Pacific Palisades, the Bay Theater and that was, that was an interesting preview because it started so weird, first the Columbia torch lady, then a title saying New York and then showing a bullfight with a high-pitched, a really high-pitched noise and then a man wakes up from a dream and the title says *Fail Safe* and I, I remembered that was one of the movies that didn't come out when it was supposed to because of, because of President Kennedy and there was a president in *Fail Safe*, played by Henry Fonda and some people I didn't know by name but I, but I recognized the faces but that's not why it was interesting, it was, it was interesting because it was the same kind of story as *Dr. Strangelove* but it, but it wasn't funny, not one thing was funny, and it was serious and scary because by mistake planes are sent to bomb Moscow in Russia just like in *Dr. Strangelove* and they can't be called back because they go past what they call the fail safe point and they can't be called back and so the President of the United States, Henry Fonda, he has to make a hard decision so the Russians don't send bombs to destroy the entire United States and his hard decision is to, to blow up New York and he does blow up New York and then it doesn't say The End it says *Fail Safe* again and the audience just sat there after it was over, before they all left. I thought it was a, a good movie and scary and tense, but I didn't think people would go see it because it wasn't funny like *Dr. Strangelove* and they already saw that one. Oh, another thing that was interesting is that there was no music in *Fail Safe*, not any music at all and I'd never seen a movie with no music at all, so that was different and interesting.

Then I saw another foreign preview at the new luxurious Lido Theater and it was, it was so much fun, another French foreign movie called *That Man from Rio* with, with, you know, writing, what mother called subtitles, and it was one of the best movies I saw in 1964. It had adventure, it was funny, they went to a lot of interesting places during the movie, the French actors were great and I wanted to marry the lead girl in it because she was so adorable and zesty. I didn't know her name until the, until the movie came out at the Fine Arts at the end of October but then I wrote it down, Francoise

Dorleac, just so I could, just so I could add her to the list of people I wanted to marry. I was fixated on the movie and saw it at the Fine Arts about fourteen times, like with *Sundays and Cybele*, and I, I followed it wherever it played and like *Sundays and Cybele* I even saw a version where they spoke English but that was, that was terrible and I'm glad I saw it only one time that way. One of the times I saw it, I took mother and she loved it for all the reasons that, that I did, but father wouldn't go because he, because he didn't want to read subtitles.

I saw, I saw other previews, like a movie called *Dear Heart*, and it was only okay good but had wonderful music by my, by my favorite Henry Mancini and Jack Jones sang the title song and I bought it on a 45 when the movie finally came out and I also bought an album called *Dear Heart* with Henry Mancini and his Orchestra and that album included the haunting theme from *Soldier in the Rain* that I, that I loved so much.

But now I just really want to talk about the last Major Studio Preview I saw in 1964 because, well, because, well, let me just talk about it. It was at the, at my favorite, the Village, and there was, there was a kind of, a kind of, I guess you'd call it a kind of excitement in the air and I don't know why and I don't really know how to even explain it since no one knew what the Major Studio Preview was going to be. Even Nate and Joe and Gary and Terrence felt it, the excitement in the air, so it, so it, it wasn't just me. I saw a couple of other preview nuts and one of them that I'd see a lot waved at me, but he never said hello or came up to me or us.

Anyway, the, the lights went down and the curtains opened and suddenly the music started and, and everyone in the theater knew immediately what that music was, including me, and then the little circles came on the screen and I knew what that meant because I'd loved the movie *From Russia With Love*, you know, that, that James Bond movie and that had, that had the same opening and so we all knew it was a James Bond movie. So, after that, when James Bond aims the gun at the audience and fires, after that the first scene started and that was like *From Russia With Love* too, starting with a scene instead of, instead of the titles.

There was a duck or a bird floating in the water near a boat but the duck or bird is fake because it's on the top of James Bond's diving suit hat and he comes up out of the water with the fake duck or bird and everyone in the theater went nuts, laughing and clapping. Then he gets out of the water and takes care of the bad guy and then he goes into a secret room and puts some kind of explosives there and a, and a timer and that James Bond music was playing and the audience was still going nuts. Then he leaves and goes back the way he came and he, he unzips the diving suit he's in and he's got on a, a white tuxedo underneath and everyone laughed and went nuts again, especially when he put a flower in his lapel.

Then he goes into a nightclub or something and there's a girl dancing and he, he lights a cigarette and then the explosives explode and then he says he has unfinished business and he goes into a room and the girl who was dancing is there in a bathtub and she gets out and they kiss and he takes off his gun and hangs it up near the tub, and then he kisses her again and behind them we see a bad man enter the room getting ready to, to, to clobber James Bond on the head with a, with a pipe or something, not a pipe you smoke, a lead pipe or something. Anyway, James Bond sees the man reflected in the girl's eye and just in the nick of time turns her around so she gets clobbered instead of him and the audience went nuts again and clapped.

Then the bad man and James Bond fight and he throws the bad man in the tub, into the water in the tub, and this is where the audience went really nuts because the bad man is close to where James Bond hung up his gun, and he's, he's almost got it in his hand to shoot James Bond and the audience is almost talking back to the movie and I'd never ever seen that happen and then James Bond looks around and sees an electric heater and tosses it into the tub, electrocuting the bad man and the audience cheered so loud they maybe heard it across the street at the Bruin Theater. And just when the audience stopped cheering, James Bond says shocking. You would, you would not believe the laugh that got and more cheering and then the main titles started and they were amazing too, with an incredible song that was the title of the movie, *Goldfinger*, and whoever the singer was she was, she was the loudest singer I'd ever heard and she never got soft, she just, she just was so loud and exciting and it was, it was the best opening of a movie ever in all my Major Studio Previews. Oh yeah, and right after they cheered when Sean Connery's name came on, the next credit said Honor Blackman as Pussy Galore and everyone laughed at that so loud but I didn't understand why they were laughing, but that, that didn't stop me from laughing too.

Anyway, the rest of the movie just got better and better and better and this was the first time anyone was seeing it, so no one had read any reviews or heard about it from people. That was one of the best things about Major Studio Previews, the excitement that you were, that you were seeing something with an audience for the very first time and there was nothing like that feeling and that's why I was fixated on Major Studio Previews, that, that feeling of being there for the first time.

The main villain, Goldfinger, was a great villain and the guy, the guy who did some of his dirty work was called Oddjob and he never said one word, he just killed people with his hat. Anyway, at the end of the movie you wouldn't believe the applause and when it said James Bond Will Be Back in *Thunderball* that got a big applause too. Of course, everyone in the audience that night wanted, well, we all wanted to have a car like James Bond had in the movie, the Aston Martin DB5 because who wouldn't want a car like that, especially with all the gadgets it had.

The next day, I looked up that car and found a foreign car dealer who handled them and I, I called and asked how much it would cost to, to buy an Aston-Martin DB5 because I'd just seen a Major Studio Preview of *Goldfinger* and James Bond drove one.

The foreign car dealer was surprised to hear that. Anyway, the foreign car dealer said that if he could get one for me it would cost $13,000, and I, I almost choked on my Swiss cheese with mustard sandwich on Weber's bread. He said there were only a thousand of them made and they were very hard to get, but he'd be happy to take my number and try to get me one and I told him that I'd have to save up for ten years and even then I probably wouldn't have enough money even though I did have $4,000 in the bank for a rainy day. So, I'd just have to be happy with my plain old chocolate brown 1953 Plymouth Cranbrook Belvedere with no gadgets.

When *Goldfinger* opened at the Chinese on Christmas Day, we decided to all go see it, mother, father, and me. We got there for the, for the 6:20 show around 5:15 and the line was practically a block long, but we got in and got decent seats and it was just as good the second time even though I knew what was going to happen and it was fun to watch mother and father's reactions and watch them laugh and applaud at things and father managed to, to stay awake for almost the entire movie. The funniest thing was when the titles said Honor Blackman as Pussy Galore and father laughed so loud and said Pussy Galore really loud, laughing and mother hit him so hard in the arm I thought he was going to fall off his seat.

We'd eaten a nice Christmas lunch at home, a chicken noodle casserole, one of mother's special dishes. But we, we were hungry after the movie but it was Christmas and nothing was open. Father drove around for a while looking but couldn't find anything so we went back to the almost house on Rexford and mother made us hot fudge sundaes without the hot fudge because she, she didn't have any hot fudge. So, it was vanilla ice cream, whipped cream, and slivered almonds and it was good but not as good as it would have been with, with the hot fudge she didn't have.

Oh, and we got a nice Christmas bonus at Wallichs Music City and Nametag Walter wished me the merriest of Christmases and I wished him the same. The last thing I bought at Wallichs in 1964, on December 30th, was the, the soundtrack record of *Goldfinger* and I listened to that on New Year's Eve over and over again until it was time to yell Happy New Year, which I did, and mother called right at midnight and yelled into the phone Happy New Year and she, she told me that father had fallen asleep like a narcoleptic on the couch and slept right through the Happy New Year.

Then it was suddenly 1965 and every year seemed to, seemed to be going by faster and faster. 1965 was an interesting year any way you looked at it or any way I looked at it, but what's really amazing, what's really amazing is that I'm about to start my seventh cassette and I've already, I've already covered so many years of Major Studio Previews, that's what's amazing. I know I left out some, but I think I've, I think I've talked about the, you know, talked about the highlights and some of the stinkers and I'll probably even go faster with the next three years because, because that will bring everything up to date, right to this year that I'm making these tapes,

1968, making this, you know, making this record of things. Anyway, 1965 was very interesting but I'll shut off the machine for now and start a new cassette for a New Year because I'm exhausted again from being yakky.

CASSETTE SEVEN

Okay, I'm, I'm back, picking up where I left off and so it was, it was 1965, a New Year and new Major Studio Previews and other things. One of the other things is that I, I turned twenty-five. Mother threw me a birthday party and, and Aunt Ida and Uncle Stu came down from where they live near San Francisco and we never see them so that was interesting because I don't think mother gets along with her sister's husband who is very, well, he's very loud and he yells at Aunt Ida if she says something he doesn't like but she yells back at him, so it's a, it's a lot of yelling when they visit.

But it was my birthday celebration and mother bought me a new baseball cap, a Dodgers cap but I only, I only want my, my Hollywood Stars cap because I, because it's, because it's part of me and I don't like, I don't like change at all. It was still very nice of mother to buy the cap and maybe someday if my, if my Hollywood Stars cap finally falls apart, maybe then I'll, I'll wear the Dodgers cap because it's a, it's a nice cap.

Mother made a pineapple upside-down cake because she knows that's my favorite, probably because I feel like *I'm* upside down sometimes with all the stuff that comes pouring out of me like everything I just said.

Anyway, it was, it was a fun party and everyone sang Happy Birthday including father who had to be shaken awake by mother because he was on the couch sleeping like a narcoleptic. After everyone left, mother sat me down, just her and me, just the, just the two of us alone. She said she wanted to have a talk in honor of my quarter of a century of living and I'd, I'd never thought of it that way, that I'd, that I'd been alive for that long but I guess I had been because I was twenty-five and sitting there.

She said you're twenty-five now and shouldn't you be thinking about maybe having a girlfriend. I thought that was a, a weird kind of question because I'd never really thought about that, not one time. I didn't, I wasn't, I mean, what girl would want to go out with someone like me who was so short and odd and loved Major Studio Previews and always wore a Hollywood Stars baseball cap and had a That's Just Harvey condition? Besides, I didn't know where you meet girls and I didn't know any girls at all and there were no girls who were preview nuts. There were a couple of girls at Wallichs Music City, I mean who worked at Wallichs Music City but they were, they would never be interested in me and to tell the truth, I would never be interested in them.

All the girls I liked were in movies and fat chance I was going to ever meet them even though I did meet Lee Remick that one time but that's just movies and not, that's not reality. I told mother that maybe not everyone was supposed to be with someone and maybe some people were meant to be alone and didn't mind it. She looked at me and then started crying but I told her it's not sad that someone is alone, not if the someone is okay with being alone, which I definitely was.

But she said she just wanted her boy to be happy and I said I was happy as long as I could see Major Studio Previews and work at Wallichs Music City and eat my Swiss cheese with mustard sandwiches on Weber's bread and my, my Campbell's chicken noodle soup and my cottage cheese with paprika. After that, I had another piece of pineapple upside-down cake and then I went home and listened to all my Henry Mancini records because it started to rain and I love rain and Henry Mancini records are the, are the perfect records to play when it rains, especially the *Dear Heart* album that had *Soldier in the Rain* on it.

Anyway, my first Major Studio Preview of 1965 was a black-and-white movie called *36 Hours* and it had a really good story that wasn't like any other story I'd seen in a movie, and it was about a German trying to get certain information from an American soldier during World War II, but it wasn't really a war movie, it was, it was about this doctor and his clever plan to make the American soldier think it was 1950, after World War II ended. They make it look like the American soldier is in an Army hospital after the war in occupied Germany. The soldier's hair has gray in it and he, he can't read without glasses, and it's all very convincing when they tell him he's had amnesia from being tortured. Anyway, he reveals everything they want to know but then realizes he's been fooled and then it gets a little hard to follow but I really liked the story and James Garner and Eva Marie Saint and Rod Taylor and that was a very good first Major Studio Preview of 1965.

Then I saw a few stinkers in a row and I was thinking that maybe 1965 wouldn't be a good year for Major Studio Previews. One stinker was called *Strange Bedfellows*, a comedy where the audience forgot to laugh, with Rock Hudson and Gina, you know, Gina whose last name I couldn't pronounce who was in *Woman of Straw*, Lolobridgeta or whatever it was.

But then, on March 5th at the Crest Theater in Westwood, I saw an IMPORTANT Foreign Preview and like *Sundays and Cybele* and *That Man from Rio* it was a French foreign movie with subtitles and it was, it was called *The Umbrellas of Cherbourg* and that made up for all the stinkers I'd just seen because *The Umbrellas of Cherbourg* was, was, well, amazing and I loved it because the music was so beautiful and everything in the movie was so beautiful and everyone in the movie sang, there was, there was no talking at all, they sang everything and if someone had told me there was, you know, that there was a movie where everyone sang everything and there was no talking I would have chosen another preview because, because that sounds like a, like a terrible idea but it was a great idea at least in French it was.

The second it began I knew I loved it because we were, we were looking down at a street and it began to rain and five umbrellas opened up at the same time, all different colors, and the music was so perfect with the, with the colorful umbrellas and the rain and of course I didn't know any of the people, the actors, because they were French and weren't in *Sundays and Cybele* or *That Man from Rio.*

I, I loved movies that weren't like other movies at all and everything, everything about *The Umbrellas of Cherbourg* wasn't like any other movie. The amazing colors, the way the whole movie looked and the, and the young lead girl was maybe the most beautiful girl I'd ever seen, at least in 1965 and of course I wanted to marry her and make mother happy and I, I would have even learned French if I married her and she liked Major Studio Previews.

Anyway, it was kind of sad at the end because the two young lovers didn't end up together but it was still beautiful and I, I hoped there would be an album of the music because I had to have it and I couldn't wait to see it again because now that I'd seen it and knew the story, I wouldn't have to, I wouldn't have to read the subtitles so much and could just watch that beautiful young girl and the pretty pictures and the rain and the umbrellas of Cherbourg. I wished I could just stay and see it again and again but Previews were only one time.

But I, I didn't have to wait too long because it opened at the Beverly Theater on March 17th and as soon as I got off work I got there for the first show at 6:30 and loved it all over again and stayed for the 8:30 show and watched it again and then I couldn't stop going to see it and I lost count of how many times over the rest of 1965 that I went. Wherever it played I went to see it and it was always in French and I never saw an English version. Mother saw it with me and she loved it too and she even saw it twice, which was, which was very unusual for mother.

When the movie opened, there was a, there was a nice ad in the newspaper and it was, it was funny because it was right next to an ad for Alfred Hitchcock's *Psycho*, which I'd, which I'd seen and was the scariest movie I'd ever seen, too scary to ever see again. Anyway, that was funny to have those two ads side by side.

The ad for *The Umbrellas of Cherbourg* said For All the Young Lovers of the World and it also said it was nominated for an Academy Award for Best Foreign Film and so I was rooting for it to win and when I watched the Academy Awards and *The Umbrellas of Cherbourg* lost, I, I wouldn't watch the rest of the show and went home and I, I never watched the Academy Awards again.

I did read the reviews and they were excellent and thought what I thought and the ad had quotes in it too and I cut out the ad so I have it here now so I could say some of the quotes in the ad. *The New York Daily News* said, "One of the Year's 10 Best!" *New Yorker* said, "Something altogether new! I applaud the boldness of concept and delicacy of execution!" *Time* said, "Demy transforms a sadly cynical musical about young love into a film of unique and haunting beauty!" The *New York Post* said, "One of the year's 10 best! You will have to see it!"

All I know is that whenever I went to, to see it at the Beverly, there were long lines and the theater was always full. I guess the young lovers of the world all wanted to see it and since I wanted to see it all the time and I wasn't a young lover of the world, I guess people who were alone wanted to see it too. Oh, I forgot, one of the reviews I read said that the beautiful girl in it, Catherine Deneuve was, well, you won't, you won't believe it because, because I didn't believe it, but Catherine Deneuve was the sister of Francoise Dorleac, the beautiful girl from *That Man from Rio*. I wondered if you could marry sisters.

The best thing was that Wallichs Music City got in a two-record set of *The Umbrellas of Cherbourg* in a, in a fold-open cover and inside the fold-open cover they had all the words they were singing in French and then in English too so you knew what the French words meant, so I bought it the second I saw it with my employee discount and a stereo version because I thought it was time for me to, you know, for me to get a nicer record player and one that was good for stereo records.

So, I told Nametag Walter that and after work he walked me to the electronics section with the TVs and stereos and he suggested two or three different ones at different, you know, at different prices. There was a Westinghouse portable stereo with built-in speakers and there was a, there was a nice Decca portable stereo and that one had speakers that came off and I liked that the speakers came off. The most expensive one he showed me was called a, a KLH Model Nineteen and it had a record player with a wood bottom and two pretty wood speakers and I, I thought that one would look nice in my, in my studio or efficiency apartment. The Decca and Westinghouse ones were half the price but I kept coming back to the KLH Model Nineteen because the other ones looked, I don't know, they looked like something a, like something a kid would have and I wasn't a kid, I'd lived a quarter of a century and was twenty-five.

Nametag Walter laughed and said he figured I'd go for the best one and I guess he knew that once I got something in my head then it was there for good. The KLH Model Nineteen was $300 plus tax but with my discount I saved twenty percent off that, so that wasn't too bad and besides all I ever spent money on was rent and movies and gas for the 1953 chocolate brown Plymouth Cranbrook Belvedere and a few things for the refrigerator like food things. So, I could afford a nice gift for my quarter of a century twenty-fifth year.

Mother came over and helped me set it up, but it wasn't hard at all. The KLH Model Nineteen sounded so amazing and it was like listening to all my records for the first time because my little cheap record player from forever ago was horrible. Even the 78s and 45s I had sounded great and mother was, mother was very impressed and I was, I was so happy I bought it. I played those two LPs of *The Umbrellas of Cherbourg* all the time and I, I loved it every time. The only bad thing was that the music that played during the titles wasn't on the album and that was, that was my favorite music.

I saw two Major Studio Previews at the Vogue in Hollywood. The first Major Studio Preview at the Vogue was called *How to Murder Your Wife* and I, I thought that one was funny and it was, it was finally a movie where Jack Lemmon was really funny again plus it had Terry-Thomas from *Bachelor Flat*, with that big space between his two front teeth. Everyone seemed to like it, me included. The second one I thought I'd like very much, *The Amorous Adventures of Moll Flanders* with Kim Novak, but it was just okay good and while Kim Novak was still pretty, the movie just kind of fell, it kind of fell flat, like a Coca-Cola that had no fizz left, like that. *How to Murder Your Wife* opened a few weeks later at the Chinese and I, I saw it again because it was playing with a, a Major Studio Preview and I went right after work and enjoyed *How to Murder Your Wife* again and then came the Major Studio Preview, and it was a, it was a Universal picture in black-and-white and it was called *Mirage* and Gregory Peck was the star.

I liked the title *Mirage*, it sounded mysterious, and the first scene was a real grabber, it grabbed me and was mysterious with all the lights going out in a high-rise building and Gregory Peck making his way downstairs and, well, it gets stranger and stranger as people keep telling him that they're surprised he's back when he doesn't think he's been away.

Anyway, I thought the story was very clever and when everything is finally explained at the, at the end it all made sense. I always enjoyed Gregory Peck and I, I liked the girl, Diane Baker was her name and I'd seen her in other Major Studio Previews, and I really liked an actor named Walter Matthau. He was really good and I knew him from that movie *Fail Safe* but that was serious and this was mysterious but had funny things too and Walter Matthau was really funny as a private investigator. But all the actors were really good and I, I liked it very much.

Another Major Studio Preview I saw was at the Beverly. And guess who was in it? Peter Sellers. Again. The movie was called *What's New Pussycat?* and it was, it was the craziest movie I'd ever seen but the audience laughed and laughed and I laughed and laughed because it was so crazy. Peter Sellers played a psychiatrist and he had long hair like a girl would have and he had, he had a German accent and I figured Peter Sellers could just about do anything and be hilarious. I can't remember all the funny things but it was two hours of funny things and I, I just knew it was going to be a big hit. Oh, and the music was so clever, by someone named Burt Bacharach, and I knew I'd be going back to see *What's New Pussycat?* and my preview nut friends loved it, especially Nate. The funny part was that when I went to see it at the Vogue where it opened a few weeks later, Nate was there too, that was the funny part and kind of a, kind of a crazy coincidence. Anyway, I dragged mother and father to see it at the other theater it was playing at, the Bruin in Westwood. I'm not sure mother loved it because it was, it was a little, a little racy, but she called it a wild ride and she did laugh a lot. I think father *did* love it because it was a little racy. He didn't fall asleep one time.

I shut off the cassette machine for a while because, because I was getting upset with myself because, well, because I have my, I have my lists of Major Studio Previews and when and where I saw them and what I thought of them, that's, that's what I've been rambling about on these cassette tapes but sometimes, sometimes I just go out of order and I don't like to go out of order but sometimes my eyes look down the list and see a Major Studio Preview from later in the year and then I just, I just want to talk about that one right away instead of going in order because I get excited and I can't help it but I'll try to help it from now on but it probably won't work because I get excited and just start being yakky about something that caught my eye but was out of order.

Anyway, I'm, I'm skipping some things too because, because I don't want to talk about every single Major Studio Preview because that's too many cassettes and too much motormouth and yakky and some of them just weren't, some of them just weren't that interesting and so to talk about them isn't that interesting.

As long as I'm out of order again, I saw a Major Studio Preview at the Beverly of a movie called, the movie was called *Inside Daisy Clover* with Natalie Wood and a lot of other actors and it took place in the 1930s and it was about a child actress who, who wanted to be in the movies and then when she's in the movies she's not happy and then things happen and she's still not happy and I thought it was good good but not a happy movie, it was a sad movie and an angry movie. I thought Natalie Wood was excellent and the movie looked excellent and I, I also liked the music by someone named André Previn and I remembered his name from other Major Studio Previews.

But the interesting part happened after the movie, that's when the interesting part happened. Oh, and I didn't mention that *Inside Daisy Clover* was a Warner Bros. movie. So, after the movie, I was, I was in the lobby with Nate and Joe and Gary and Terrence, talking about the movie and whether the audience enjoyed it. Anyway, out of the blue a man comes over and taps me on the, on the shoulder and I didn't know who it was but before I could even say hello he said are you Preview Harvey and that was weird and out of the blue. I said yes, that's what Jerry Lewis called me and Blake Edwards too and a, and a man from M-G-M and a man from Paramount and he said he'd heard all about me from the M-G-M man, who he was friends with. He said he was with Warner Bros. and he, he asked if he could talk to me. So, I, I said goodbye to my preview nuts and the man from Warner Bros. and I went to a corner of the lobby.

He said everyone thinks you have a good ability to know what audiences will go to and what audiences will stay away from. I didn't know how to answer that because it wasn't, well, because it wasn't really a question. I said I just guess at it and he said but how and I said I don't know how it just, it just comes to me. He said what did you think of *Inside Daisy Clover* and I, I stood there trying to, trying to figure out what to say. He said I don't want you to be nice or kind, I'm interested in what you thought, and I want you to tell me from the heart, what you thought and what your instinct is about the picture.

I said good because I, I can't fib about things, I can't fib and say I loved something if I didn't, you know, love it. He said I understand, go on and I said well, I thought it was good good. He said what does good good mean? I said good good means it wasn't great good, it was good good and that was better than okay good or a stinker. I didn't think it was a stinker but it's, it's a sad movie and an angry movie and I'm not sure if people want to see sad and angry movies. He said so you think people won't come, even for Natalie Wood and I said I thought she was, I thought she was wonderful in it and the movie looked good and the music was good and I did enjoy it, but I just didn't, I just didn't, I just didn't... He said just didn't what? I said sorry things get jumbly in my head and sometimes I can't, I can't, sometimes it takes me time to, to put things into, into words. Anyway, I told him that I didn't think the audience response was, was, I didn't think they en joyed it and maybe they thought it was, it was just okay good.

He said thanks for being honest. He said we're all a little worried about it but we're hoping the star power of Natalie Wood and Christopher Plummer, he's hot off *The Sound of Music*, and even Robert Redford, who's been getting a lot of attention lately, we hope that will bring folks in. It opens just before Christmas at the Pantages.

I didn't know if I should, if I should say anything, but he, he said he wanted an honest opinion so I said I don't know if, I don't know if people will want to see a sad and angry movie about an unhappy girl who's treated so, who's treated so poorly and used by everyone, I don't know if people will, will want to see that when it's Christmas and people just want to be festive and happy.

He said I truly hope you're wrong, but I fear you may be right and not just with audiences but with critics. We'll know soon enough. I said I hoped I was wrong too but I didn't say that I didn't think I was. He said I hope to see you at more previews, because sometimes talking to real movie fans face to face is better than reading preview cards.

He said it was nice meeting you Preview Harvey and you're getting a bit of a reputation with all of us. I wouldn't be surprised if more studios ask for your opinions.

We shook hands and he walked away and I just, I just, I just stood there for a minute, trying to, trying to remember everything he'd said. I hurried to my car as fast as I could so I could, so I could write down what he'd said because, because no one had really said anything like that to me before, at least not those words.

As soon as I got home, I, I called mother and told her about what the, what the Warner Bros. man had said and she said it was well deserved and that it should make me feel very special and I told her it did and she said good because you are.

It started to rain while I was, while I was driving home and then, and then I remember sitting in my one chair and hearing the rain hit the windows and roof and I, I remember putting on my *Dear Heart* Henry Mancini record and playing the *Soldier in the Rain* music on my new stereophonic record player while I listened to the rain and when that music would end I'd just, I'd just move the needle back and play it again while listening to the rain and reading all those things the Warner Bros. man had said to me in the lobby.

I'd never had anyone ask what I, what I thought about anything, except mother and father. Not one person. No one cared what a 5'3" turtle in a Hollywood Stars baseball cap thought about anything. But now, people from three different Hollywood studios, Paramount, M-G-M, and now Warner Bros. were, were actually interested in hearing me, Preview Harvey, hearing me tell them what I, what I thought about their movie. I'd never felt special in my whole life, that I, that I had any value or worth, but maybe now, maybe now I felt just a little bit special and I, I liked that feeling, I liked that feeling very much.

I think I'll stop now and continue at some point tomorrow because I, I have to turn the tape over soon anyway and I want to just, I want to just put on the Henry Mancini *Dear Heart* record and play the *Soldier in the Rain* music and imagine it's raining and remember how I, how I felt that night.

Okay, I, I flipped the tape over and I, I may as well admit that I, that I took yesterday off from the cassette machine because when I got through with work I went to a Major Studio Preview and I can't, I can't wait to be yakky about it but I'm still at the end of 1965 and I don't want to talk about a 1968 Major Studio Preview when I'm still talking about 1965 Major Studio Previews.

Anyway, now I'm going back in order and I, well I probably shouldn't even talk about the next two Major Studio Previews but I have to, I have to talk about them because I have to because they were interesting, but I'll try not to, not to be too yakky about them too much because they were also stinkers. The first Major Studio Preview was at the Stanley Warner Beverly Hills and was an M-G-M movie called *The*

Sandpiper and everyone in the theater was excited when it said Richard Burton and Elizabeth Taylor and I was excited too because I knew they were, I knew they were big movie stars even though I'd never seen them in a movie. I thought it was funny, well, not the movie, the movie wasn't funny but I, I thought it was funny that excitement can go away so fast and be replaced by wanting a movie to be over. Not only that, but the audience, the audience was laughing at things that weren't funny and that was bad because you knew it wasn't good that they were laughing at things that, that weren't funny. The movie was really a stinker and you could, you could feel that in the theater.

Richard Burton and Elizabeth Taylor weren't at the Major Studio Preview but a big movie star was and that was fun to see everyone trying to, trying to get near her. It was the woman from *Mary Poppins* and *The Sound of Music*, Julie Andrews. I didn't see Major Studio Previews of those, but I saw them when they came out and liked them and everyone liked Julie Andrews and I didn't know, I didn't know why she came out to see a Major Studio Preview of a movie she wasn't in. I stood off to the side and just watched her and she seemed so nice giving autographs and smiling for photos when people with cameras were screaming "JULIE! OVER HERE!" She seemed like a, like a very nice person.

Unfortunately, the M-G-M man was there and unfortunately he came over to me and asked me what I thought of the movie and not to fib. I said are you sure and he laughed and said well now I know what your reaction is, but let's hear it. I said it was kind of a stinker, sorry. He said do not be sorry, never be sorry for not enjoying something. We're hoping Burton and Taylor will pull them in but we think that critics will kill it. I said that I did like the music and he said he did too. I was kind of hoping he'd, that he'd take me to meet Julie

Andrews but he didn't. When I left, she was still there waving to people and, and signing autographs.

The other Major Studio Preview was at the Village and that was always my favorite place to see a Major Studio Preview because everyone was so nice to me. All us preview nuts came to see a Cinemascope and Color by Deluxe Major Studio Preview and we all knew it was going to be, to be a Twentieth Century Fox movie because that was the only studio that still said Cinemascope and Color by Deluxe. Oh, and the, the movie playing there was called *A Thousand Clowns* and I, I got there in time to see it and I liked it very much and all the actors were good and the little boy was, well, the little boy was short like me and he said lots of, of funny things but there weren't a thousand clowns on the screen so, so that was confusing.

Anyway, the Major Studio Preview began and hearing that music that played when it said A Cinemascope Picture was always exciting and I couldn't wait to, to see what the movie was. Right away a small airplane tried to land and, and it flipped over and caught on fire and that was a good way to start a movie. The first name on the screen was someone I never heard of, Max von Sydow, but the second name was Yvette Mimieux and I loved Yvette Mimieux and wanted to marry her. When the title came on it said Serge Bourguignon's *The Reward* and then I was really excited because, because Serge Bourguignon was the, he was the director of *Sundays and Cybele* and of course that was one of my, one of my favorite movies.

One of the other actors was Nino Castelnuovo and I, I knew that name from all the times I saw *The Umbrellas of Cherbourg*, because he was, he was in that, so that was exciting too. So, I, I don't like to, I don't like to say it but I have to say it because I'm, I'm making a record of things and so

I'll just say it was, it was maybe the biggest stinker ever in the history of stinkers and how could that be when it was the director of *Sundays and Cybele*, one of my favorites in the history of movies, so that was weird and I, I didn't understand it at all. I was surprised that it was, that it was over at around 10:00, which meant it was only ninety minutes long because it seemed like it was, like it was three hours long.

A lot of the audience walked out during the movie and went home and my, my fellow preview nuts said they hated every minute of it and I guess, I guess I figured out that directors didn't always make good movies. It just made me want to see *Sundays and Cybele* again.

Another Major Studio Preview I saw was called *Repulsion* and I thought that was a really good movie and a couple of times it was so weird and creepy and disturbing that it made me, it made me jump out of my seat a couple of times like when hands suddenly came through walls, that was disturbing, hands coming out of walls, but the whole movie was weird and creepy and disturbing. But the best part was, the best part was that the lead girl was Catherine Deneuve from *The Umbrellas of Cherbourg* and she, she spoke in English in *Repulsion* and looked so beautiful but she was playing a girl with, with a condition or mental problems and by the end of the movie she's killed a nasty man by slashing him to death with a, with a, you know, with one of those old-fashioned shaving razors and she's totally crazy and I guess they take her away and, and put her in a mental institution. That was a good movie, and even though, even though she had mental problems she was still beautiful and I still wanted to marry her unless she had a razor.

The last Major Studio Preview I saw in 1965 was at the Stanley Warner Beverly Hills. It was an M-G-M picture in black-and-white and Panavision called *A Patch of Blue* with

Sidney Poitier and introducing Elizabeth Hartman. It was about a blind girl whose mother is a, well, you'd have to say she was, she wasn't like mother, this mother was a mess of a mother and she was, she was, well, mother would have called her a loose woman and she was horrible to her blind daughter and the blind daughter's grandpa was not any help at all because he was, he was always drunk like in *Days of Wine and Roses* but worse.

One day in the park she meets Sidney Poitier and he's nice to her when she's scared of a storm that happens and he meets her there and they, they become friends and he helps her string beads and to find a bathroom when she, when she needs it and they always have a nice time and he, he tries to help her because she isn't educated or anything. But then the nasty mother finds out about the nice man and finds out he's a Negro and then she gets even meaner but the nice man, Sidney Poitier, arranges for the blind girl to go to a, to a school for the blind. It was very touching and the music was so pretty and Sidney Poitier was so nice and gentle and Elizabeth Hartman was so good as the blind girl and I, I would have helped her too if I'd known anyone like that, and I just loved the whole movie.

All the preview nuts were there and they all liked it and Terrence really liked it because, because he said it portrayed Negroes in such a positive way and that Sidney Poitier was such a, such a good role model. The M-G-M man was there and he found me and asked what I thought and I said this is a great picture and the blind girl is so good but so are all the other actors, and it's, it's touching and beautiful and I loved the music too and I hope there's an album I can buy and I think, I think everyone will love it. He said can't ask for better than that, Preview Harvey, and let's hope everyone agrees with you and I said they will. He seemed very happy and he patted me on the, on the back and said glad you were here and hopefully we'll see you at the next one and I said you will.

When *A Patch of Blue* opened at the, at the Crest in Westwood, I went and saw it four more times and loved it each time. I cut out some reviews and they were all excellent. Oh, and I now had a, a nice box of all the things I'd, that I'd cut out of the newspapers, like reviews, Major Studio Preview listings, and anything else that I thought was, that I thought was interesting. I wish I'd thought of, of doing that a long time ago, that would have been fun. Anyway, it looked like I was, like I was right about the movie because there were, there were long lines to get in to see it.

I couldn't believe how fast the year 1965 had gone but it was, it was almost over and I was a quarter of a century old and I finally thought I had some, I had some, you know, some value and worth because some studios wanted to, to know what I thought. Oh, and we, we got a nice bonus again at Christmas from Wallichs Music City so I bought mother and father something they really needed and the store wrapped it up pretty with a, with a red bow on top, and I, I brought it over for our usual Christmas dinner.

Mother made her famous ham. I always, I would always ask why is it famous and she'd, she'd say I can't reveal that, it's a secret and it wouldn't be famous anymore if I told you. Father would groan and say not that again, what are you, Mrs. Henny Youngman, take my wife, please. Then we'd all laugh because, because that was our little routine that we did whenever she made her, her famous ham that nobody knew why it was famous. She also made her famous candied yams that she only made with her famous ham so she could say we're having a ham and a yam jam. She'd been saying that since I could remember and we laughed and laughed. That would, that would always get another groan from father and he'd say why don't you two go on Ed Sullivan?

For our Christmas dessert she made her famous lemon meringue pie that was, it was very lemony. The meringue was confusing and I, I never understood what the, why it was, why it was there because it just tasted weird but I guess you couldn't call it lemon meringue pie unless you, unless you had the meringue part even if it was confusing and tasted weird.

Then we all exchanged presents and I got, I got mother and father a new General Electric Chrome Toaster Oven and when mother unwrapped it and, and saw what it, when she saw what it was, she said oh, my Gawd, Hahveeeeee, this is too much, this cost too much. I said you need a new toaster and this is, this is also a toaster oven and did lots of other things and that their toaster was from 1952 and only made burnt toast. Father looked at it and said so I don't have to eat burnt toast anymore? I said that's right, this makes perfect toast every time, but like I, like I told mother, you can make other things in it too, it says right on the panel. I pointed to where it said things on the, on the panel. I said see, you can make meatloaf or a baked potato or frozen dinners and, and things like that.

Mother said this is amazing, but you shouldn't waste money buying us things. Father said why shouldn't he, we're all going to the poorhouse anyway, spend it if you have it. Mothcr and fathcr gavc mc a wonderful present to hang on my wall. I, I, I had no idea where she could have, where she could have even gotten it but there it was in front of me in a nice frame, a poster, a, a movie poster, a real movie poster from *Sundays and Cybele*, the kind they have in front of the theaters. I was flabbergasted and said where did you, where did you get this? She said with a, with a twinkle in her eye, I have my ways.

She followed me home in her car and she brought a hammer and nails and a, and a thing to hang the poster on because I didn't, I didn't have a hammer and nails and a thing to hang the poster on. We decided where to hang it and then she hung it for me because I would have, I would have put fifteen holes in the wall trying to, you know, trying to get it right. I couldn't believe I had a real movie poster and from, from one of my favorite movies, right there on my wall where I could look at it every single day and night.

Mother said enjoy it in good health and then she, she went home and I put on the soundtrack to *A Patch of Blue*, which had just come in at Wallichs Music City and I'd grabbed it right up and I sat in my one chair and just, and just stared at the movie poster of *Sundays and Cybele* and I bet no one else anywhere had one but mother had her ways and somehow, somehow she managed to, to get it for my present.

Then it was, then it was 1966 and I yelled Happy New Year at midnight like I, like I always did, and mother called right after that, like she always did and said Happy New Year and we all hoped it would be a Happy New Year and I hoped that 1966 would have lots of wonderful Major Studio Previews to see. I, I remember I fell asleep in the chair looking at my new movie poster hanging on my, on my wall. It's still there and I'm looking at it while I'm making this record of things on this, on this cassette machine and I, I still love my poster along with my Blake Edwards and Henry Mancini autographs and also, well, I'll save that for when it, for when it actually happened and I, I guess I'll, I guess I'll start a new cassette for 1966.

CASSETTE EIGHT

Okay, a brand-new cassette and a, a brand New Year, 1966, and more brand new Major Studio Previews to see, and lots of, lots of other interesting things.

My first Major Studio Preview of 1966 was a, it was at the, at the Pantages where *Inside Daisy Clover* was still playing. In the ad it said this was a Major Studio PRESS Preview in Panavision and Technicolor. I went right from work and I, I sat through *Inside Daisy Clover* again and I couldn't believe it but there were only, there were only eight people in the whole theater and it was, it was a very big theater. But it filled up for the Major Studio PRESS Preview and the other preview nuts were there and we talked before the, before the movie, wondering what we were going to see. Nate asked us if we, if we, well, he told us he was going to Los Angeles City College now and taking theater classes. He was shuddering or jerking like crazy when he was telling us so when he invited us to, to come see him in a play all I could, all I could think of was how would he get through a play if he was, if he was shuddering and jerking like that and making utterances? But we all said we'd come and he said he'd arrange tickets for us for the, for the following Thursday night.

Anyway, we all, we all took our seats and then the movie started and it was Warner Bros. The first thing that we saw was Paul Newman waking up when his alarm clock goes off. So, everyone was, everyone was very excited it was Paul Newman waking up. The name of the movie was *Harper* and there were lots of famous actors in it. Anyway, the opening was funny with Paul Newman getting ready and having to, to use an old coffee thing from his trash, I think a filter or something, I didn't know because I didn't drink coffee and I still don't drink coffee. Then he puts on a gun and leaves and his door says Private Investigations, so we, so we know right away he's a private detective. I liked private detective movies and I, I really liked *Harper.* It was funny and suspenseful and all the actors were good, and the, and the ending was a surprise, at least to me it was. You could tell the audience loved it and it got a nice applause at the, at the end.

After the movie, us preview nuts were in the lobby. They enjoyed it as much as I did and Nate gave us all the, the address of Los Angeles City College to see him in the play. I saw the Warner Bros. man but he was busy talking to people who were, who were probably the press or something. But as I was starting to leave he, he saw me and came over and he smiled and said well, what did you think? I told him I thought it was great and had a good story and I, I liked everything about it and I thought it was going to be a big hit. He said that's just what I wanted to hear. I'll pass your comments around because everyone is interested in what Preview Harvey has to say. I'm, I'm not sure I, I'm not sure I believed that was true or not that everyone was interested in what, in what I had to say but it was a nice thing to hear. He told me that *Harper* was, was opening in a few days right here at the Pantages.

When I, when I got to the car, I wrote down my favorite line in the whole movie. "Only cream and bastards rise." That one got a big laugh from everyone, including me. I called mother and told her all about the movie and I said that line to her and she said they're allowed to use language like that in a movie now? I said I didn't think that that "B" word was such a bad curse word and she said still, in a movie?

Oh, before I, before I talk about another Major Studio Preview, I want to talk about the play we saw Nate in at Los Angeles City College because it was very interesting. Even though I was a quarter of a century old and about to even be older in a couple of months, I'd, I'd never, I'd never seen a play. The four of us preview nuts, me, Joe, Gary and Terrence met at the, at the theater building on the campus and there were quite a few people there to see the play. Joe was wearing his usual suit and was upset they didn't sell buttered popcorn at the theater and Terrence looked like he always did, serious and neat and tidy and Gary had some interesting yellow art stains on his shirt and I asked him what they were and he said, he said the stains were mustard and the, and the art was called Mellow Yellow on a Starched White Shirt.

We went to the box office and Joe got our tickets that Nate had left for us and then we went in and got our seats. They gave us what they, what they called programs and thc play was called *Mother Courage*. The lights went down, just like, just like in a movie theater. There was a curtain, just like in a movie theater too, but instead of parting to the sides it went up and there were, there were people on the stage and they began speaking in very loud voices, I guess to, to make sure everyone could hear them. I tried to understand what they were talking about but I, I couldn't figure it out.

There were platforms all over the stage and that was interesting but not as interesting as Nate when he finally came on. He had some, some talking parts and that was the, that was the interesting thing because while he was onstage doing his part and talking and moving around, he never had his, his, you know, his condition. He never jerked or shuddered or had any, any out of the blue utterances. I couldn't figure it out and I couldn't figure the play out and it was a, it was a long play full of loud talking.

After the play, we met Nate in front of the theater and he was jerking and shuddering like crazy. I, I didn't want to, to ask him why he didn't do it in the play, but I thought he, he probably doesn't want to be asked that and so I didn't. I did tell him I didn't understand the play and he said, he said he didn't either and he was in it and we all laughed. Joe and Gary and Terrence told Nate he was good and so did I and Nate said he was, he was very glad we came to the play even if nobody understood it.

I saw a Major Studio Preview at the new luxurious Lido called *Lord Love a Duck* and it was a crazy movie and it was, it was all over the place and I think it was, I think it was supposed to be a comedy but it wasn't funny, not that I could see, and *The Sandpiper* got more laughs even though they didn't want laughs because it wasn't a comedy. I, I didn't understand why anyone in the, in the movie was doing what they were doing but I didn't care because the star of it was Tuesday Weld and she was still beautiful and so adorable so I still wanted to marry her no matter how big a stinker the movie was. When it opened at the Vogue a week later it got, it got very bad reviews that also thought it was too all over the place and, and not funny. I cut out the reviews because they, they all had pictures of Tuesday Weld.

Okay, I just want to say, just because I'm making a record of things, I just want to say that right around that time I, I, I don't know why, really, but I was looking at my, my old coloring books from when I was young and how I colored outside the lines and I liked seeing them, they were from such a, such a different time. But while I was, while I was looking through them a photo fell out of one of them and it was, it was a photo of me and Pearl and I, I hadn't thought of Pearl in a long time and that made me sad and I wondered why I hadn't thought of her in a, in a long time. I put on some sad music, *Soldier in the Rain* was the saddest music I had, even sadder than *Days of Wine and Roses*, and I looked at the photo and she, Pearl, she looked so happy and we were both smiling and I had hair and didn't look like a turtle yet.

I thought, I thought Pearl would be around eighteen now and I bet she would have been, I bet she would have been so pretty and happy and why did she have to, have to, you know, why did she have to die when she hadn't even really lived yet? Why was that fair? I remember looking at my, at my *Sundays and Cybele* poster and how sweet Cybele was in that movie and it made me think of how sweet Pearl was and I just wanted to see her again, just one more time because everything happened so fast that she was there one day and, and gone the next and I didn't get to, I didn't get to say goodbye to her.

I called mother and the second she heard my voice she said what's wrong? I told her about looking through the old coloring books and the photo falling out of one of them and mother was just silent so I, so I asked her don't you ever think about Pearl because I can't, I can't remember us ever talking about her. Mother was quiet for a minute and then she said she didn't talk about it because she knew how sad it would make me and she didn't like to see her boy sad. She said when you lose a child you don't forget about them, you think about them every day and not one day has gone by when she hadn't thought about Pearl, not one day.

I felt bad about not thinking about Pearl but I know it would have made me feel sad all the time if I did and I don't think, I don't think Pearl would have liked that, for me to be, for me to be, you know, sad. Anyway, I just wanted to say that, to have it be a record.

But like mother always said, laughter is good for what ails you and that was so true because, because my very next Major Studio Preview was at the Bruin and it was in black-and-white and Panavision. The first name on the screen as soon as the movie started with, with exciting music was Jack Lemmon and you could hear everyone in the theater was happy, and the second name on the screen was, was Walter Matthau and I, I remembered him from that movie *Mirage* and he was so good and funny in that so I knew he'd be so good and funny in this one too, and the movie was called *The Fortune Cookie* and it was the, the same director as *Some Like it Hot*.

Anyway, in the first scene Jack Lemmon is a cameraman at a football game. I don't like any sports at all so I, I hoped the whole movie wasn't going to be about football. Anyway, a football player is running and trying to keep away from the other players and he's running and accidentally knocks over Jack Lemmon and his, and his camera. Anyway, I won't go on too much about it but Jack Lemmon's injuries were not bad at all but his, his brother-in-law is known as Whiplash Willie because he makes his clients pretend to have bad injuries so he can, so he can collect big on the insurance. He convinces Jack Lemmon to go along with it and he does. There are lots of funny complications and every time Walter Matthau opened his mouth the audience roared with laughter and so did I.

I did it again, I went out of order again, why do I keep doing that? *The Fortune Cookie* was later but just, just thinking about it made me laugh so I jumped the gun and I, I went out of order again. So, backing up, I, I saw a Major Studio Preview at the Vogue in Hollywood and it was, it was Debbie Reynolds in *The Singing Nun*. Mother and I had already seen a singing nun in *The Sound of Music*, and that was still playing at the Wilshire, so this was another singing nun and it was a weird movie with Debbie Reynolds singing songs and playing guitar and riding a motorbike and one of the songs she was singing she sang over and over again, it was called "Dominique" and it was, it was the most annoying song I'd ever heard but Debbie Reynolds as *The Singing Nun* kept singing it and helping everyone and some other nuns didn't think she should sing anymore and I didn't think she should sing anymore and then a person who went to a church and said they were pregnant and were going to, to have an abortion and I wondered what movie I was watching and then they sent *The Singing Nun* to the Congo to help people and I was glad she went to the Congo so I wouldn't have to hear her sing "Dominique" anymore and then it was the end of the movie and I couldn't wait to leave and even though the M-G-M man was there, I snuck past him, which is, which isn't hard when you're 5'3" and a turtle.

When *The Singing Nun* opened at the Beverly a few weeks later, we got in the soundtrack album at Wallichs Music City and I didn't buy it because I didn't want to hear The Singing Nun sing "Dominique."

But here's a Major Studio Preview I did like and I was excited to, to find out what it was because the ad for it said Tonite! Come Early! Top Stars! It's a Big One! So, right after work, I drove immediately to the Picwood to see whatever the Top Stars! It's a Big One! was. *Thunderball* was playing there, the James Bond movie but I'd seen it at the Chinese and liked it, I liked it but not like I loved *Goldfinger.* I sat through the last thirty minutes of it and, and found an okay seat but not the one I, I liked. There wasn't a, a long intermission and the theater was filled so I, I didn't get a chance to talk to my other preview nuts, but they were all there and we waved to each other and a couple of other preview nuts were there and the one who sometimes waved at me waved at me and I, I waved back.

Anyway, the curtains opened and music began and it was a, it was a Universal Picture and then it said Paul Newman and the audience clapped and then it said Julie Andrews and the audience clapped and then it said Alfred Hitchcock's *Torn Curtain*, so that was exciting because I liked Alfred Hitchcock movies and I, I liked Paul Newman and Julie Andrews. The story was good and there were lots of good scenes and Paul Newman and Julie Andrews were kissing a lot until he treats her badly and lies to her because he's on a, a secret spy mission to get secrets and find out things and she follows him and things get messy, but he, he has a job to do. A German policeman follows Paul Newman to a farmhouse and there's an amazing scene where, where Paul Newman and a woman who's trying to help him have to kill the policeman and it was, it was really hard to kill him but they finally do and the audience clapped when that scene was over. There were other exciting scenes and a cute ending and I, I wanted to see it again right away whenever it opened.

Paul Newman and Julie Andrews weren't there so I just said hi to my fellow preview nuts and they loved the movie too, but we, but we all loved Alfred Hitchcock movies and Paul Newman movies and Julie Andrews movies and we all thought the murder scene was great.

Oh, and at that preview I met a man from Universal and that became another studio that had heard about Preview Harvey and that made me feel good and, and mother thought so too when I told her. She said soon all the studios will want your opinions and won't that be something. It *would* be something if that, if that happened and it did but not yet so I'll wait to talk about that when it did happen, because it was, it was, well, I'll talk about it later.

Some other Major Studio Previews I saw after that I won't, I won't spend too much time on because now I only, I only want to talk about the important ones or the ones that were, that were really special. So, a Major Studio Preview I saw at the Wiltern was called *The Trouble with Angels* and Hayley Mills was in it and I'd seen her in other movies and liked her and it was another nun movie but there were no singing nuns and that was a relief and I liked the movie, it was funny.

At the Village I saw a Major Studio Preview called *Fantastic Voyage* and that one was weird where they made people tiny and put them in someone's body so they could save them or something like that. I thought it was, I thought it was a little silly because you can't make people tiny and put them in someone's body but I enjoyed it anyway, just because I'm, I'm tiny in real life just not as tiny as they were. Stephen Boyd was in it, I liked him in *The Third Secret,* and someone named Raquel Welch who scared me and I don't know why, I just thought she was scary and I didn't want to marry her.

At the Pantages I saw a Major Studio Preview called *Big Hand for a Little Lady*, a, a western movie with Henry Fonda in it and it was about, it was about poker but I didn't know anything about poker but I liked Henry Fonda and I liked Joanne Woodward who was the Little Lady who had the Big Hand. After the movie, Joe, who was still eating his big box of two-squirts of butter buttered popcorn said that Joanne

Woodward was married to Paul Newman and I, I didn't know that.

At the Village again I saw a Major Studio Preview of a movie called *Gambit* with Shirley MacLaine and Michael Caine and that one had the cleverest beginning where the whole first thing you're watching for twenty minutes or something like that, the whole story you're being told is, it isn't real it's a, it's a story being told and then the real movie starts and it's a robbery picture and I really liked it because the beginning was so clever. When the movie came out the poster said, "Go ahead and tell the end but please don't tell the beginning" and I thought that was a funny way to tell people not to, not to give away the trick at the beginning even though I just did.

Oh, and I turned twenty-six and mother and father took me out for a special birthday dinner and it was, it was special because, because I got to choose the restaurant and after talking to Nametag Walter at Wallichs Music City, he said I should choose a place where I've, where I've never been and I said that I walked by the Brown Derby a million zillion times and I always wanted to, to go there but I didn't think you could wear a, a Hollywood Stars baseball cap in there so I never went and he said that's where you should go and just tell your mother to call and explain that you wear the cap because you have a rare skin condition and I thought that was a great idea and that's what I chose and mother did call and say I had a rare skin condition and they let me wear the Hollywood Stars baseball cap.

First, mother and father came to Wallichs Music City to get me. We had reservations for 5:30 at the restaurant. They'd never been to Wallichs Music City since I, since I started working there. Nametag Walter came and got me when they asked for me, since he was at the main counter. Nametag Walter said to mother and father it's so nice to meet you, Harvey has told me so much about you. Mother said and he's told us so much about you. Nametag Walter said your son has been such a godsend here, in my estimation we don't have a better worker than Harvey. I was, I was just standing there listening back-and-forth like a, like a tennis match, and my face felt all I guess you'd say hot or flushed or something and I was probably, I was probably red as a tomato.

Nametag Walter said you have fifteen minutes left, why don't you show your parents around the store? So, that's what I did, even though they'd been there before, they, they really hadn't seen the whole store, just where the records are. I showed them the listening booths and how I filed listening copies and where we put the new copies that people could buy, then I showed them the electronics department with the radios and stereos and TVs. Mother looked at the Sylvania Oriental console twenty-five-inch color TV and she said to father maybe it's time we get a color television, look how pretty the colors are, so lifelike and vivid and I just read an article in the *TV Guide* that said everything's coming up color and that over half the TV shows will be in color now and father said sure spend my money like there's no tomorrow only there is a tomorrow and I don't want to be in the poorhouse when it comes and mother told him to be quiet he was making a scene and besides they were married and therefore it was *their* money not his money and he said fine we'll come back on the weekend and buy a color television if it'll shut you up and she said if we have a color television I'll be watching it all the time and I won't have to shut up and he said good and that was that.

I'll jump ahead, just because I'm making a record of things and I, I don't want to forget. So, they did come back on the weekend and bought that Sylvania Oriental console twenty-five-inch color TV but father was happy because they gave him my employee discount off the $700 price and he saved $140 but then he complained when they added the 3% sales tax and that was going to put him in the poorhouse.

Anyway, after the electronics department, I showed them the sheet music department and the musical instruments department and then it was, then it was time for me to clock out, so I did that and then mother and father said goodbye to Nametag Walter and I did too, then we left the store. Father looked across the street at the Home Savings Bank and put his hands on his hips and said when did they get rid of the NBC Studios? I told him it was two years ago and that it was horrible how noisy it was when they were, when they were tearing it down and he said look at that thing they replaced it with, that's disgusting and mother said take your hands off your hips, Spartacus, and let's go eat. Just out of the blue like that mother could be so funny and I laughed when she said Spartacus because we'd all seen that movie at the Pantages with reserved seats and father had come out of the movie and said why did everyone keep saying they were Spartacus in that movie, I'm Spartacus, no I'm Spartacus, I'm Spartacus, when we all had been sitting there for three hours and we all knew Kirk Douglas was Spartacus so who would believe all these other people were Spartacus?

Anyway, we walked the block to the, to the Brown Derby. It was only 5:20 so we, we went across the street and looked at the Huntington Hartford Theater, which I walked by practically every day but had never been in. Mother said touring shows played the Huntington Hartford and sometimes they had big stars in them. I still had a bad taste in my mouth from seeing the play *Mother Courage* so I wasn't that interested in ever seeing a play again. We looked at the, at the poster for what was playing there and it was a, a play called *The Typists and The Tiger*, well, it said two one-act plays but I didn't know what that meant and it said they were hilarious plays and that the stars were Eli Wallach and Anne Jackson. Mother said I'd know Eli Wallach if I saw him because he'd been in quite a few movies. I thought it was funny that, that someone named Wallach was so close to Wallichs Music City down the street, even though there was, there was a one-letter difference, although lot of people thought Wallichs was Wallachs even though all the big signs said Wallichs plain as day.

Then it was 5:30 and we went back across the street and went into the Brown Derby. Mother spoke to the person who greeted us and then we were seated in a very nice booth and no one said anything about my Hollywood Stars baseball cap. Everywhere on the walls were, there were drawings and mother said those were all the celebrities that had eaten there and that was, that was amazing, all those drawings of celebrities that had eaten there and I even recognized several of them.

They gave us menus and we all read them. I had no idea what a lot of the food was so I asked mother what was good to have. I mean, I knew spaghetti but the menu said Derby Spaghetti and I didn't know what that meant but mother said that just meant it was their special way of making spaghetti. She pointed to the left side of the menu at the top and said this is the dish they're famous for. So, I, I read the dish that they were famous for, which was called a Cobb Salad, and it, it said "Often Imitated, Never Duplicated, this distinctive salad is our Pride and Joy, A delicate finely chopped fresh salad greens, avocado, peeled tomato, crisp bacon, chicken, hard cooked egg and Danish bleu cheese, tastefully tossed with our old-fashioned French dressing."

Since I'm making a record of this, I, I don't want anyone to think I still remember what was written two years ago on a menu, although I'd, I'd probably be close. No, I made mother write it all down so I'd have it as a memory. It sounded like something I'd like, so that's what I ordered. Mother said you're always safe ordering a specialty of the house or their pride and joy. Mother ordered it too. Father never liked to do what anyone else did so he ordered the Brown Derby Steak Sandwich on, on sourdough toast with onion rings, french fries, and Derby Slaw.

While we waited, mother told me that Clark Gable had proposed to Carole Lombard here and Cary Grant ate here and *I Love Lucy* did a whole episode here and she said we should, we should keep a sharp lookout in case, in case a famous person came in.

Anyway, the food arrived and mother was right about the, about the Cobb Salad signature dish, it was so good and she, she loved hers too and I ate every single bit of it and even wiped up the dressing on the plate with bread, that's how good it was. Father said his steak sandwich, which was going to put him in the poorhouse, was very good and he ate it all and all the onion rings and french fries too. Mother kept a sharp lookout for famous people but she didn't see any. Father paid the bill and we left without seeing any celebrities. But I was, I was so happy to have eaten at the Brown Derby after all those times of walking by it and the, the Cobb Salad was so good.

Later, we all drove back to mother and father's house, not together, I mean, they took their car and I took mine. She'd made the usual birthday treat, the pineapple upside-down cake and we all had a piece of that and it was as good as always. Then mother gave me my birthday present, two nice wool sweaters, some, some pullover shirts, and two pairs of nice pants and I needed clothes so that was, that was good and I wouldn't look so, my clothes wouldn't look so worn out because I, I just wore the same things over and over again and, and never went shopping for clothing. It was a nice birthday and I was, now I was twenty-six. I went home and hung my new clothes in the, in the closet and mother had given me a piece of pineapple upside-down cake to take home and have for lunch the next day, but I just, I just put on a record, the soundtrack to *A Patch of Blue* and ate it right then because, because That's Just Harvey.

Okay, I'm back, I was hungry and I had a Swiss cheese sandwich with mustard on Weber's bread, some Campbell's chicken noodle soup and some, some cottage cheese with paprika on it and I read the movie section to see if there were any Major Studio Previews, but it was, it was one of the times when there wasn't a single Major Studio Preview. Well, there was a single one but it was in Downey and I didn't, I didn't even know where Downey was.

Anyway, I guess, I guess I'll talk about my favorite Major Studio Previews from the rest of 1966, just three movies, because I saw, I saw some stinkers and some okay good previews and I, I'm bored of talking about those right now. So, the weirdest one I saw was really a different kind of movie and it was disturbing but I really liked it and I, I thought it was haunting and strange and just, well, just different. I saw it at the Regent Theater in Westwood, a new theater I'd, I'd never been to, just a half-block down from the Village. It was a very small theater and kind of, kind of plain, like really plain, more like the new luxurious Lido and my othcr preview nuts weren't there because they probably chose one of the, one of the bigger theaters that had a Major Studio Preview that night, but I wanted to, I wanted to see what the Regent was like so that's what I chose, the Major Studio Preview at the Regent.

The Major Studio Preview was in black-and-white and it was A Paramount Picture so that always made me happy.

Then there was kind of, I guess you'd say eerie or scary music and the main titles started and they were weird and creepy and I'd, I'd never seen any main title that looked like that. It was like, it was like, I can't even say what it was like because I don't know how to, but there was this weird effect and then a big eye and it said Rock Hudson and people didn't applaud, they booed when it said Rock Hudson and I'd never heard that either, booing a name. Then it was, it was almost like the eye or the image becomes, I don't know, almost becomes gooey and it was really, well, weird, that's the, that's the only word I can think of. Then it said in the John Frankenheimer film and then there was this distorted mouth and the title of the film was in the distorted mouth and it said *Seconds*. Then there was scary organ music and it, it put me very on edge because it was so weird and I honestly did not know what I was in for because the rest of the titles were all over these gooey, distorted face images. Then it said music Jerry Goldsmith and he'd written the music for *A Patch of Blue* but this was, this was nothing like that, this was, this was creepy and disturbing.

Then the movie started and I can't even describe what I was, what I was watching but it was a strange man following an older man to his train and even though, even though nothing was really happening it was kind of scary, I don't know why. Anyway, when the man gets to his train the man who was following him calls him by name and puts a piece of paper in his hand and then the scary organ music plays again. I know I'm being a motormouth and yakky about it but I, I just want to, I just want to say how weird it was.

Anyway, the movie is about this middle-aged man who seems unhappy and bored so he goes to a company that gives people a second chance at life by, by arranging for them to be officially dead even though they're not dead, and then they have surgery and get a new face and new identity and this, this second chance at life. The middle-aged man does it and turns into Rock Hudson and then he, he ends up not being happy with his new life and he wants a third chance at life but he doesn't get a third chance at life because they, they finally end up killing him by drilling a hole in his head and that's the end.

Oh, and there was one scene in the movie where they went to a kind of, a kind of festival where they got in a big thing like a big tub and stomped grapes to make wine or something like that and everyone took off their clothes when they did that and you could, you could see naked parts that I'd never seen before in a movie and that was kind of interesting.

I think about half the audience walked out, but those of us who were left were kind of just, kind of just sitting there in shock and then we all just got up and went to the lobby. The Paramount man was there and he came right up to me and said I was hoping I'd see you, what did you think? I really didn't know how to, how to put it in words because I'd never seen a movie like that, but I said what I thought, I said I really thought it was interesting and like nothing I've ever seen and I've never seen Rock Hudson like that and everyone was good but it was the whole feeling of it that I was just, I couldn't look away and the story was so interesting, so I have to say I really liked it a lot but I don't know if anyone else will and I, I don't think it will, I don't think audiences will come see it even though they should and sorry I know I talk like a motormouth but I just want to say I thought it was a great movie.

He kind of smiled a, I don't know, a sort of smile and he said yep, you hit the nail on the head, Preview Harvey, it's a really good film but it's too arty and we don't know how to sell it or even tell people what it is. I've seen the ad campaign and between you and me and the projection booth, the ads wouldn't make you want to see it.

I said maybe it's one of those, one of those movies that people will, maybe they'll discover it later. He said yeah maybe they will someday but I think we're basically just dumping it citywide on a double bill. He said but I'm really happy you liked it because I like it too and I hope you don't mind if I tell everyone at the studio what you said and that includes the director, Mr. Frankenheimer because he's very proud of the movie. I said I didn't mind at all.

When *Seconds* came out a couple of months later, I saw the, I saw the ads in the paper and the Paramount man was right, they were terrible and didn't really, they didn't really tell you what the movie was about and they put it on a double bill with a western called *Waco*. I'm glad they released it though and I went to see it again at the Hollywood Theater and it was just as creepy and disturbing and I liked it even more, and I was, I was just about the only one in the theater. But somehow the scene where they were all stomping grapes and, you know, being wild and naked, well, that scene was, was shorter and didn't have the parts where you could see the really naked parts and I thought that was interesting. Anyway, I'm, I'm glad I saw it a second time because who knew if they'd ever be showing it again.

The second Major Studio Preview that I loved I saw at the Picwood Theater. I hadn't, I hadn't seen the movie it was playing with, *Kaleidoscope* with Warren Beatty, so I got there in time to see it and I liked it quite a lot especially Susannah York, who I wanted to marry because she was so cute and had such a nice smile and teeth.

At the intermission us preview nuts were yakky and caught up. It was always funny to see me holding my box of Dots and, and Joe holding his, his two squirts of butter buttered popcorn but there we were and that never changed. Terrence told us that he got into UCLA and he was so happy about it and we were all happy about it too because it was, it was so important to him and he was going to be a teacher because that's what he always wanted to be, a teacher. Gary had on a beige shirt and it had a kind of, a kind of pink round stain on it and he called it grapefruit on a beige shirt. I asked him once how he could make his shirt stain art and then wash the shirt and it would go away and he said art is ephemeral and I didn't know what ephemeral meant but it, it sounded good. Mother told me ephemeral meant fleeting and I understood fleeting but not ephemeral.

Anyway, we all got in our seats and then the movie began and it was a Columbia picture in Technicolor and Panavision. The title came on fast and it was called *The Professionals* and then there were quick scenes of all the actors as their names came on and they were some of my, my favorite actors, first Lee Marvin then Robert Ryan then Woody Strode who I saw in *Spartacus*, then Burt Lancaster, then some other actors I, I didn't know by name until it said Claudia Cardinale, and that name I remembered from, from *The Pink Panther* and I remembered she was beautiful, and it was a very exciting way to open a picture and the music was exciting too and it was a western.

So, this, this rich person hires the professionals to find his wife because she's, she's been kidnapped by a bandit and rcvolutionary and if they bring her back he'll pay a big reward. So that was the story and the whole movie was so much fun and entertaining and funny and dramatic and the audience reaction was so loud and Claudia Cardinale was so beautiful and of course everything was not exactly as it seemed because she wasn't really kidnapped she wanted to be with the bandit and didn't like her rich husband so much, and the professionals let her go and then the rich husband turns to Lee Marvin and says, he says you bastard and Lee Marvin looks at him and says yes sir, in my case an accident of birth. But you, sir, you are a self-made man. I never heard an audience at a western laugh so loud and cheer and that was the end of the movie and the audience applauded and cheered and I, I knew this was going to be a big hit movie and when it opened a week later at the at the Pantages it was a big hit movie and I went and saw it three more times and it was, it was just as good every time and the audience reaction was always the same.

I wrote down the B-word line when I got back to the car and I called mother later and told her I heard the "B" word in a movie again and she said movies are changing and I guess they can get away with anything nowadays. She was shocked when I'd told her about that, you know, that grape stomping scene in *Seconds* where everyone was not only naked but you could see naked parts you'd never seen in a movie before at least I hadn't seen them and she said she didn't need to see anybody's naked parts but her own.

Anyway, *The Professionals* and *Seconds* were two of my favorite movies of 1966. The other movie that was a favorite Major Studio Preview in 1966 was a crazy movie at the Crest in Westwood. I didn't get there in time to see the movie playing there, *Alfie*, because Nametag Walter asked me to stay at Wallichs Music City and work an extra two hours and I would do anything for Nametag Walter so I did because it was December and everyone had already started their holiday shopping and it was always the busiest time of the year for Wallichs Music City.

So, right after I finished I, I clocked out and drove all the way to Westwood and got there just in time and as I, I rushed into the lobby I saw the Warner Bros. man so I knew it was a Warner Bros. picture we were going to see. I rushed right into the theater and got the seat I liked so, so that was good and I, I looked around and I saw Nate and Joe and Gary and Terrence and they came and said hi and then we had to take our seats because the movie was about to start. Oh, and I told them I saw the Warner Bros. man and so it was a, it was a Warner Bros. picture.

So, the movie started and we were in, we were in some huge library and the camera was going down an aisle towards a big double door and I, I knew it was a camera because when it got close to the big double door there was this, this huge shadow of the camera on the wall and I'd never seen that in a movie before, a huge camera shadow on the wall in a movie. Anyway, while it's going toward the big double door there's silence like in a library because you're not allowed to be yakky in a library, you have to be quiet in a library. Suddenly, the double door opens and a song starts playing, a catchy song with a, with someone singing it, like a rock-and-roll kind of song, and there's the blind girl from *A Patch of Blue*, only she's not blind and she's in color and she's just walking down the aisle like she owns the library and the title of the film is *You're a Big Boy Now*. Her name came on the screen, Elizabeth Hartman, and then other names like Geraldine Page, who I knew from, from *Toys in the Attic*, and a silly name Rip Torn, who I didn't know, and other names I didn't know, except for Julie Harris who was in the Major Studio Preview of *Harper*.

Anyway, it was a crazy movie with crazy characters but I really liked it because the main character in it was short, not short like me, but short and there's a girl who likes him and he likes her but he likes Elizabeth Hartman more and he's, he's fixated on her, and I, I understood being fixated and she's crazy because one minute she's being sweet and loving and letting him move in with her and the next minute she's being really mean and awful to him and the next minute she's fine and then she's mean and awful and it was, it was funny and wild and the audience seemed to really like it because it was so, well, different and weird. I'm glad I didn't know anyone like the girl that Elizabeth Hartman played because that would have been awful and it made me glad I was, that I was on my own.

I told the Warner Bros. man that I really enjoyed the movie and I thought that young people would really like it because it had rock-and-roll music and catchy songs and it was funny and he agreed that he thought the young people would go for it and that it was opening in a couple of weeks at the Fine Arts on Wilshire in real Beverly Hills for a one-week run for Academy Award Consideration, but then wouldn't be released until March of 1967 at the Bruin. I loved when they, when they told me things that no one else knew and I, I always, I always kept it to myself. Oh, and I guess I should say there were some naked parts in *You're a Big Boy Now* because the short main character sees a bunch of of naughty magazines and you can see the covers and I was surprised that you could, that you could have that in a movie. I didn't tell mother about that part because she, she didn't want to know about naked parts in movies.

Anyway, this cassette is, this cassette is almost full so I guess that's it for 1966 other than it was kind of, kind of the typical Christmas and I, I worked overtime and got more money and I spent Christmas with mother and father and it was the same as always and New Year's Eve was the same as always and that was my life, the same as always and then it was already 1967 and I'll, I'll start a new cassette for 1967.

CASSETTE NINE

Okay, I started a new cassette for, for 1967. I just want to, I just want to say that I, I can't believe I'm almost caught up to when I'm making these cassettes, you know, 1968. It feels like I've been a motormouth and yakky and talking nonstop for, well, for a couple of months now and I, I guess that's right, I guess I have been. That's a lot of yakky but when you're, when you're making a record of things then that's what happens. Depending on how, on how yakky I am on this cassette, this cassette could come right up to the time I began making this record on cassette tapes.

Before I talk about some Major Studio Previews I saw in 1967, I want to say that having made all these tapes, well, one of the, one of the most interesting things was seeing how things, seeing how things change.

When I started going to Major Studio Previews when I was fourteen, I loved the big Cinemascope and stereophonic sound movies, those were the, those were the most exciting for me back then. But then things started changing, and I, I guess I started changing too because I started seeing smaller Major Studio Previews and even previews that weren't from studios at all and I was, well, it was interesting that I began to love those kinds of movies, those, those smaller movies too like *David and Lisa* and *Ladybug Ladybug*, and also foreign movies, well, French movies anyway, at least the ones I saw at IMPORTANT Foreign Previews. I still loved the bigger pictures too, but even those began changing and they were different from what I'd, from what I'd seen and I liked those different movies and I also began to know that not all movies were good and some were stinkers and I, I thought it was good to know that, to know that not all movies were good and some were stinkers and I guess my point is that things changed and I guess I changed even though I was still 5'3" short and a turtle and Preview Harvey, but I didn't really like change but I liked certain kinds of change and that was interesting and I guess I just wanted to say that to have, to have a record of it because in 1967 things changed too and so now I guess I'll talk about some of the Major Studio Previews I saw in 1967 but I won't talk about all of them because like before some aren't even worth talking about unless they were such stinkers that it's fun to talk about then I might talk about them but I probably won't because there's too much else to talk about and I've been talking for a couple of months already and as mother asked last week, is the novelty wearing off, and I said no but I'm, I'm tired of hearing myself talk into the cassette microphone so maybe the novelty is wearing off but I want to finish it because that's what I set out to do and when I become fixated on something I have to, I have to finish it because, well, That's Just Harvey and I've already said that a million zillion times so let me just talk about the first Major Studio Preview I saw in 1967 at least according to my list.

It was a Major Studio PRESS Preview at the Pantages. I loved when there were Major Studio Previews at the Pantages because I could just walk up there from Wallichs Music City. They were showing a movie called *Any Wednesday* and it was, it was okay good but not good good. The Major Studio PRESS Preview was a movie called *Hotel* and it was about a hotel in New Orleans and I, I didn't know where that was but it looked interesting. Rod Taylor was the star and a new girl I didn't know, Catherine Spaak, she was pretty and I wanted to marry her because while some things change, some things *never* change, and there were other actors who I'd seen in other movies.

Anyway, it wasn't like the crazy newer movies I'd been seeing, it was old-fashioned and that was, I don't know, that was nice for a change and I loved the whole movie and so did my fellow preview nuts, especially Terrence since there was stuff about Negroes and what Terrence called bigotry in that part of the country. The music was really good too and there was a hotel thief that was funny but all the characters were interesting and there were so many stories, not just one story, so that was interesting and the Warner Bros. man was there and I told him it was a wonderful movie and that I thought it would be a hit and he said he was delighted to hear it and when I left the theater I noticed that the poster was up and it was coming soon and I hadn't noticed the poster on my way in.

The other Major Studio Previews I saw after that for the next couple of months they were, they were all stinkers and I had never seen so many stinkers in a row and the worst stinker was called *Oh Dad, Poor Dad, Mamma's Hung You in the Closet and I'm Feelin' So Sad* and with a title like that you'd, you'd think it would be funny but it wasn't funny at all it gave me a headache and I got out of there so fast that I, I didn't see the Paramount man.

The next Major Studio Preview I liked was at the Village and it was a musical movie and I, I hadn't seen one of those in a long time and it was called *How to Succeed in Business Without Really Trying* and it was really funny and I liked the songs and all the actors, especially Robert Morse as the main character, he was really funny and there was a really funny song about a coffee break and one called "I Believe in You" that Robert Morse sings to, to himself in a mirror, that was funny but the whole thing was funny and I liked the girl in it, Michele Lee was her name.

After the movie, I was outside the theater and saw that Michele Lee was there and she was laughing and people were congratulating her. The manager came up to me and asked me if I wanted to meet Michele Lee and I said yes because I did want to meet Michele Lee and he took me over to her and said Miss Lee this is one of our best customers, he's at all the Major Studio Previews here and everyone knows him as Preview Harvey and he just wanted to tell you how much he enjoyed the movie and you.

Michele Lee looked over at me and smiled her cute smile and said Preview Harvey what a cute name and I said I really enjoyed you in the movie and it was so funny and I'll buy the album for sure because I work at Wallichs Music City and anyway, I just thought you were great. She thanked me and shook my hand and the whole way back to the car I kept, I kept smelling my hand because whatever perfume she was wearing I could smell it on my, on my hand. I told mother about it and she wanted to see it so I said we'd go whenever it came out but it didn't come out for almost two months.

We did go when it came out at the Chinese and she loved it as much as I loved it but I was confused because the funny number about the coffee break wasn't in the movie anymore and they must have removed it for some reason and that was interesting that they'd change something after a Major Studio Preview.

Then there were a bunch more Major Studio Previews that were stinkers and I didn't, I didn't understand how there could be so many stinkers in a row but there were. Oh, before I tell you about the next Major Studio Preview that I loved I guess I should tell you that my, my wonderful 1953 chocolate brown Plymouth Cranbrook Belvedere died. It just died one day with no warning, it just stopped working. Well, I guess there *were* warnings because it made funny noises and sometimes smoke would come out of the back and sometimes it was hard to start so I guess those were warnings. So, anyway, on the day it died it, it wouldn't start and mother called the Automobile Club of America for me and they came and towed us to the gas station we liked and they said the car was dead, it would need a completely new engine and it wasn't worth it to spend that kind of money on a dead car because that wasn't the only thing that needed to be fixed and the best thing would be to, to get a new car. I was very sad that my car was so dead and I wished they could make it work again, but they couldn't and I didn't know, I didn't know about cars so much and what to buy but mother said father would help figure out what car and help with the cost and the gas station said they'd give me two hundred dollars for parts, so mother and I said okay and they gave me two hundred dollars for parts.

Having to get a new car was the kind of change I, I didn't like, I didn't like that kind of change so father looked in the paper at the car ads and since he was the one who found me the 1953 chocolate brown Plymouth Cranbrook Belvedere I told him that I only wanted a Plymouth Cranbrook Belvedere but he found out they didn't make that anymore but that they had three other kinds of Plymouth Belvederes and the one that sounded best was called the Plymouth Belvedere Satellite. The price for a brand new one was around $2,695, but father found a used one from 1965, only two years old and he, he said it had low mileage, was in excellent condition, and was $1,400.

I had two hundred dollars from the old car and father said that even though it would put him in the poorhouse we could, we could split the other $1,200 and he'd pay half and I'd pay half and that would be my birthday present and so that was what we did. Anyway, the car dealer let us take a test drive and it drove like a car so we gave him a check and I had a brand new used two-year-old car and it only had 9,000 miles on it and it was a very nice gold color and it didn't make noises or have smoke coming out the back and was easy to start. When mother saw it she said it looked, she said it looked very sporty so it was nice to have a very sporty car and she said I looked sporty in it.

The first Major Studio Preview I drove my sporty new used car to was at the Bruin in Westwood. I couldn't get there in time to see the movie that was playing, *Two for the Road*, and I'd have to, I'd have to see that another time because Audrey Hepburn was in it and she was one of my favorites. The Major Studio Preview ended up being a wonderful movie, another Warner Bros. picture and the title was, the title was *The Family Way* and it had Hayley Mills in it and I didn't know any of the other people, but it was, it was an English movie that took place in England and it was about newlyweds and their problems because they have to live in the young husband's family's house with his mother, father, and brother, and that makes everything difficult. But it was a, it was a wonderful movie and the young husband's mother was, I don't know, she reminded me of mother a little, I don't know why, since she wasn't really like mother, but she cared about her son like, like mother cares about me. It had a naked part in it too and that was, that was interesting because of who did the naked part and that was Hayley Mills and I'd seen her in some Walt Disney movies, so it was a big surprise to see her naked, well, not all of her, just a little of her behind, but still she was all, she was all grown up now and so that was interesting.

Anyway, I told the Warner Bros. man how much I liked it and he said he was happy I did and I said I think it's going to be a hit and he said he thought I was spot on and I didn't know what that meant but it sounded like spot on was a good thing and it was because it *was* a hit and I saw it five more times when it was playing at the Crest and I cut out some of the reviews and ads for it. Oh, the music, I really liked the music and that was a surprise because it was by, it was by Paul McCartney, he was a Beatle and I liked some of the Beatles' songs but his music for the movie was just music and no songs. So, that was a very good Major Studio Preview.

Some albums we got in at Wallichs Music City that I bought right away were *You're a Big Boy Now* because I liked the songs and there was a really pretty theme that was just music no singing called "Amy's Theme." I bought the soundtrack to *How to Succeed in Business Without Really Trying* and I, I played that a lot, and I bought *The Family Way* by Paul McCartney and listened to that one a lot too.

Anyway, I'm, I'm only going to talk about three more Major Studio Previews from 1967 just because, because I loved the three Major Studio Previews and because the three movies were my favorites of 1967 with my other favorites I'd already seen and that I've already talked about, and the other Major Studio Previews I saw besides these were either good good or okay good but I just want to talk about these three because they, they were the ones I really loved.

So, let me talk about the Major Studio Preview I saw at the, at the Chinese and it was another one of those, another one of those times when there was something in the air, some excitement in the air like the Major Studio Preview of *Goldfinger* at the Village, that kind of excitement in the air. The Chinese was still playing *How to Succeed in Business Without Really Trying* and so I went right to the theater after work because the ad said IMPORTANT Major Studio Preview! Top Stars! Color! Come early! So, I came early and sat through *How to Succeed in Business Without Really Trying* for my third time and I enjoyed it just as much but still missed the song about the coffee break.

All us preview nuts were there, the ones from our group and the few others and there was no time for talking because everyone was in their seat waiting, although we waved to each other. I'd already eaten all my Dots during the first movie and I wished, I wished I'd saved a few for the second movie. Then I became fixated on that I didn't have any Dots left so I asked the man next to me to please save my seat and he said he would and I ran to the candy counter and because it was only three minutes from the Major Studio Preview starting, there wasn't a, there wasn't a line and I got a new box of Dots and then I, I ran back to my seat that the nice man had saved for me and just in the nick of time too as those beautiful red curtains started to part and the lights turned off.

Then the M-G-M lion came on and roared so it was an M-G-M picture. Then there were soldiers and I wasn't happy about soldiers because I, I didn't like war movies and now I was, I was stuck seeing a war movie. Then a prisoner is going to be hung and Lee Marvin was there and I liked Lee Marvin so that was okay, at least. Then they hung the prisoner and then there was another long scene where Lee Marvin is given an assignment by Ernest Borgnine and I liked Ernest Borgnine so that was two okays even if it was a war movie. His assignment was to train twelve prisoners who are sentenced to die or to, or to be in prison for years, train them to kill Nazis and if they, if they survive the mission, they'll be pardoned.

Anyway, then Lee Marvin meets the twelve prisoners and the titles finally begin after ten whole minutes of no one knowing what movie we were seeing. First, the title came on and it was *The Dirty Dozen*. The audience applauded Lee Marvin's name, and some of the other cast too and it was a really amazing cast, at least the ones I knew, like Robert Ryan and Ernest Borgnine and Charles Bronson and George Kennedy. I recognized the director's name, Robert Aldrich, because at one of the Major Studio Previews I saw at the Wilshire the movie playing there with it was *What Ever Happened to Baby Jane?* and he, he directed that movie and that was a really good creepy and weird movie that I loved.

So, even though I hated war movies and I, I couldn't wait for it to be over, I did like the actors. Anyway, I was, I was so wrong because I loved the movie, and it was so funny and so clever and then so exciting at the end and the actors were amazing and the audience reaction was just as crazy as it was for *Goldfinger*, with laughing and cheering and a big applause at the end of the movie and I thought this was going to be a big hit movie and I couldn't, I couldn't wait to see it again even if it was a war movie and I hated war movies but not *The Dirty Dozen*.

Everyone leaving the theater was talking about how great it was and it was so crowded in the lobby that I couldn't wait to get out where the footprints were. Everyone was, was standing around talking and our group of preview nuts was talking and saying how much we loved the movie and then I saw the M-G-M man and I went over to him and tapped him on the shoulder and he turned and said hi and said to the people he was talking to this is Preview Harvey, he goes to lots of previews and he always seems to know which pictures will be hits and which won't. I began being yakky but I, I couldn't help it and I said this is maybe the best Major Studio Preview I've ever seen and I think it's going to be a big hit, a big, big hit because it was funny and exciting and had good action, it had everything and I can't believe it was two-and-a-half hours long because it, it didn't seem like that long because it was so entertaining and maybe I better stop because I could go on and on because I have no off button but I hate war movies and I wanted to, I wanted to leave when I saw it was a war movie but I'm glad I didn't because it was so entertaining and I loved it.

I finally was able to stop being yakky and they all thanked me for my opinion and said to spread the word and I said I would spread the word. They went back to talking to each other and I'm sure, I'm sure they didn't know what to make of me being yakky like that. The M-G-M man turned to me and said I wanted them to hear it from you because no one gets more excited at a good picture than Preview Harvey. He said they couldn't have been happier with the audience reaction and he told me it was opening in just two weeks across the street at the Paramount and then he, he gave me a card with his name and phone number on it, an M-G-M card, and he said to call him if I wanted to see it again and he'd, he'd arrange for passes for me.

When I got home, I called mother and could barely stop talking about *The Dirty Dozen* and she said she didn't know if the movie was for her but I said if I hate war movies and I loved it then you might love it too and I think father will really love it, so she said okay that we could all see it. So, I called the M-G-M man and a woman who worked for him said our names would be at the door, not the box office, and we didn't, we didn't have to wait in line so we all went and saw it on a Friday night and the line must have been two blocks long but we went right up to the door and went right in the theater and got the best seats.

Oh yeah, I turned twenty-seven and I had dinner with mother and father and had the usual pineapple upside-down cake and mother said look how old my boy is, time sure flies, and father reminded me that I'd, I'd already gotten my birthday present and I said I remembered that because I'd driven over in it and mother had already commented that the birthday boy looked sporty in his new used sporty car.

I was thinking, I was thinking, well, I'm twenty-seven and, and what do I have to show for it? So, I made a list. I thought, I have a good job at Wallichs Music City to show for it and just look at all the Major Studio Previews I've seen and how many interesting people I've met and Jerry Lewis nicknamed me Preview Harvey and the studio people all asked me what I thought of their movies and Mr. Edwards told me I was his, his lucky charm, so I guess, I guess I had something to show for it, for being twenty-seven, even if I was the only one who knew it.

So, the next Major Studio Preview I want to talk about was, I saw it at a new theater in Westwood, another, another small theater like the Regent and this one was called the Plaza and I wanted to see what it was like and so I, I went to a Major Studio Preview there. It was about three-quarters full and my other preview nuts weren't there, they were probably at a bigger theater Major Studio Preview, and I, I don't know why but I had a hunch that this would be a good Major Studio Preview. I got there ten minutes before the preview started and since it wasn't totally full I, I got the seat I liked and I had my Dots and then the preview began.

So, the movie started and it was Warner Bros. again, but kind of a brown color on the WB shield thing, like, kind of like an old photo brown color. Then there were some photos and the sound of, a sound like a camera snapping a photo or something, old photos and then it said Warren Beatty and the people in the audience booed just like they booed when Rock Hudson's name came on in *Seconds*. I didn't mind Warren Beatty and I, I didn't understand what Warren Beatty had ever done to them that made them boo in a movie theater. Then more photos and a name I didn't know, Faye Dunaway, then more photos and more names I didn't know and there was no music, just the camera snapping sound until what sounded like a really old, a really old record was playing. And the title of the movie was *Bonnie and Clyde* and I didn't know why a movie would be called that.

Anyway, after the titles were done it said who Bonnie and Clyde were, that Bonnie Parker worked in a café before beginning a life of crime and Clyde Barrow who already had begun a life of crime and had already been in jail. I won't talk too much about it because I just thought it was a, a great movie and everyone in it was great and interesting and there was an actor who got kidnapped in it who was so funny and the audience laughed a lot at that scene and by that time in the movie I, I guess they forgot that they booed because they all loved the movie. But the thing I want to say is, the thing I want to say is that it was so, the killing in it was so real with so much blood and I'd never seen that in a movie. After a robbery, Clyde shot someone hanging onto his car, he shot him right in the eye and they, they showed it, and then at the end when Bonnie and Clyde get shot up it was so long and so many bullets and in slow motion and regular motion and lots of blood everywhere and everyone just sat there and after that the screen went black and then it just said The End and everyone just sat there and couldn't move, just like with *Seconds*.

After the movie was over, I saw the Warner Bros. man and, and I told him I thought it was great and that all the people who booed Warren Beatty sure changed their mind and loved the movie and he, he laughed at that and said he thought that was funny too and I told him the most interesting thing was that it was so entertaining but also that the bad people are the stars of the movie and I, I don't know how, but you kind of, you kind of like them and hope they'll get away with everything and he said that was what was unique about the movie. I told him I hoped it would be a big hit and that I thought it would surprise people and that it would be a hit and he said right, that's called word of mouth and I didn't know what that meant but he said it's when people tell other people it's a movie they have to see, and that's what everyone was counting on.

I told mother about it, well, I told mother about all the Major Studio Previews even if they were stinkers, and she thought it sounded interesting but didn't know if it was for her but I said she should see it and we all did and she did like it but was surprised like me that you could, that you could like two people who killed other people. Anyway, all the reviews I read said it was the best picture of the year and I cut them out along with some big ads, oh, and it was a big hit movie that had, that had word of mouth.

Oh, and two other things that happened in 1967 and I, I couldn't believe it but I guess I should because it happened. Someone from Columbia came up to me at a Columbia preview and said everyone at the studio knew who Preview Harvey was and that he wanted to meet me because I was such a fixture at previews and had good movie sense. Mother was very impressed that so many studios knew who I was and we would have told father but he'd gone out like a light, as mother put it, watching *The Andy Griffith Show.*

So, the last Major Studio Preview I want to talk about was another Warner Bros. picture and another favorite movie of 1967 and Warner Bros. was really having a good year as far as I was concerned. Mother and I went to the Picwood to see the Major Studio Preview and it was called *Up the Down Staircase* and was about, it was about a woman teacher teaching in a bad high school and I didn't know any of the actors except for the teacher, Sandy Dennis, because I saw her in *Who's Afraid of Virginia Woolf?* that was playing with a Major Studio Preview I went to. The movie was so real and funny and moving and dramatic and the kids all seemed like, they all seemed like real kids not actor kids and there was one character, a girl who was, who had a, I guess had a crush on her English teacher and he was mean to her and she couldn't deal with it and she, she tried to kill herself and that was my favorite part, not that she tried to kill herself, that was sad, but that she was so good in the part and made you love her even though she wasn't pretty or anything, and the English teacher who was mean was so good in his part, especially when he got fired. Oh, and I loved the music, which didn't sound like other movie music at all and I, I can't even say why it was different but it was. Sandy Dennis was wonderful in the movie too and I'd never seen any other actress like her before, she was so, well, mother called her quirky. Anyway, I loved the whole movie and so did mother and I was, I was surprised they didn't play it in one theater, it just opened in a bunch of theaters and I went to see it again and it was playing with *Hotel*, so I saw that again too. When we got the album to *Up the Down Staircase* in at Wallichs Music City, I bought it and played it a lot because it was so different than other movie music. Oh, but the best thing about the preview of *Up the Down Staircase* was Terrence after the movie when mother met the other preview nuts and Terrence said that's what I want to do, to make a difference like that teacher did, and I, I bet he was going to be a great teacher and make a difference.

Mother liked all the preview nuts and said she was happy to meet them and they, they liked her too and she especially admired the brown stain on Gary's blue shirt that he called Chili Dog Blues.

Oh, okay, there was one other Major Studio Preview I'll, I'll just mention because it was great and, and you won't believe it but it was, it was another Warner Bros. movie and it was called *Wait Until Dark* and my favorite, Audrey Hepburn played a blind woman like in *A Patch of Blue* and she was tormented by bad people who think she has something they want and it was so scary and the main bad guy was so creepy and weird and disturbing and Henry Mancini wrote the scary music and there was one scene at the end where, where someone you think is dead suddenly leaps out from the dark because they're not dead and I think the entire audience jumped out of their seats and I jumped out of mine and everyone screamed so loud and then, and then all the lights are out on screen and they, they turned out all the EXIT signs in the theater so it was totally black in there and it was so suspenseful and, well, I loved it so I'm glad I didn't forget to mention it.

And I guess that's about it for 1967 other than the usual things like Christmas and New Year's Eve and then it was 1968 and that's when I'm, that's when I'm making these cassette tapes, this record of things that I thought should have a record. My idea is to stop here because I think I've said about all I can say and I think that's plenty because I'm a motormouth and yakky.

So, before I turn off the machine, I just, I just want to talk about the Major Studio Preview I saw a couple of weeks ago but then I said I'd wait to talk about it and now it's time to talk about it. Of course, it was at the Village and that was, that was always like going home for me and everyone said hi and my Dots were ready for me and our preview nut group was there and the other couple of preview nuts, including the guy who always smiled and waved at me and we all got our special seats and then the lights went out and the curtain opened.

Then it was, it was some kind of desert scene and men were marching in skirts and blowing on, I think it's called bagpipes, they were blowing on bagpipes, and then we see people with guns waiting to ambush them and there was one person trying to get to the top of a hill so he could, so he could blow his trumpet and warn all the marching people blowing on bagpipes and he does and then he's shot and falls down blowing the trumpet but he keeps getting up and blowing it again and we were, we were all starting to laugh and then every time he'd get up and blow the trumpet he was shot more times by more people and the laughter just got louder and louder and it went on and on and on and he just won't die and keeps blowing his trumpet even though he's just been shot a million zillion times already.

Then we see it's a movie being filmed and the producer is, he's yelling at the director that it was his idea to bring this trumpet-blowing actor over from India. Anyway, we finally see the Indian actor is Peter Sellers and he, and he causes more trouble on the set and they finally fire him after more funny things happen and by that time we were, we were all screaming with laughter and we didn't even know the title of the movie yet.

Then the title finally came on and it was *The Party* and I, I didn't need to see it was A Blake Edwards Production to know that he was the director and I already loved the movie. Anyway, Peter Sellers accidentally gets an invitation to a Hollywood party from the producer of the desert movie and he goes and from that point on there was, there was no story at all and it all took place in the house where the party was and it was laugh after laugh after laugh until I, I almost couldn't breathe and tears were running down my face. The whole entire audience was, they were laughing like that from start to finish and it got a big applause at the end.

I wondered if Mr. Edwards was there. I hadn't seen him since, well, since 1964, I think. I didn't have to wonder very long because the manager of the Village came and found me and he, he said Mr. Edwards wanted to know if you were here and I told him you were and he wants to see you.

So, the manager took me over to where Mr. Edwards was and the manager said I found him, Mr. Edwards, and Mr. Edwards turned around and looked at me with a big smile on his face and he said for God's sake, Preview Harvey, where the hell have you been? You're my good luck charm and boy did I need you on my last three pictures because they all kind of tanked and I think it's because we didn't have the Preview Harvey seal of approval. So, I hope you liked *The Party* because I need a hit, and then he laughed.

I said it was maybe one of the funniest movies I'd ever seen and he said thank God, we have the Preview Harvey seal of approval and maybe this thing will be a hit and I said I knew it would be because it was, because it was so funny and I was crying I was laughing so hard. He said is there anything better than hearing a big audience all laughing together at the same time and I said that was the best thing. He told me to give my phone number to his assistant so he could, so he could make sure I was at every Major Studio Preview for a movie he made. I gave his assistant my phone number and Mr. Edwards patted me on the top of my Hollywood Stars baseball cap and said I see you still have your cap and I said I did and that I was, I was never without it because of That's Just Harvey and he didn't know what That's Just Harvey meant but he laughed anyway and I didn't explain that it was a condition.

Anyway, that, that seems like a good place to stop because I'm all caught up to right now in 1968 and I've made nine cassettes already and that's a nice record of things on cassettes. I don't, I don't know why it was so important to me to do this, but it was and so I did it and now if anyone ever wanted a record of things they'd have it although I couldn't think of anyone who would want a record of my Major Studio Previews and other stuff about mother and father and poor Pearl and my group of preview nuts and Nametag Walter and Wallichs Music City. I mean, I, I didn't know who would care about those things but I'm glad I did it even though it took a long time and a lot of being yakky into this cassette machine microphone.

So, I'll, I'll, I'll just keep going to my Major Studio Previews and I'm sure there will be lots to go to and I'll work at Wallichs Music City and I'll see mother and father and I'll get older and that's my life, that will always be my life and I'll always be Preview Harvey because that's who I was, that's who I was meant to be, I guess. And even though I have no, no off button, this cassette machine does, so I'm pushing the off button now.

AFTERWORD

That was the end of the tapes, or so I thought. Just before assembling all this, I was going through Harvey's box of review clippings and ads. Sitting on top of the clippings was his cassette recorder and I'd put that on the floor while I looked through the review and ad clippings in the box, which I have to say were fascinating. As I was putting the cassette player back in the box, I noticed there was still a cassette in it. I rewound it and played it. There wasn't that much on it, just a few things he'd recorded sporadically over the next few years. I thought it was important to include that because it kind of completes the story in a way, and while I could certainly complete *some* of the story in a dispassionate way, I think Harvey should have the last word, in his own unique voice and his own unique way. I do hope some people get some enjoyment out of this and I only wish you could hear the tapes themselves. Well, there's always an audio book, I suppose.

So, for one final time, once again, I give you Preview Harvey in his own words.

N.G.

CASSETTE TEN

Testing, testing to see if, to see if this machine still works.

I guess it does. I, I haven't used this cassette machine since, since 1968, when I, when I finished making my, making a record of things on cassettes. I just wanted to come back and say that I've seen lots of great Major Studio Previews in the past few years, but last night was so interesting that I thought, I thought I needed to make a record of it because it was, it was so interesting and I still had one new cassette tape I hadn't used.

So, I, I guess I should say it's 1974 now and maybe I should say that we still have our group of preview nuts, although we don't, we don't see Terrence as much because he's a teacher now at, at University High School in Westwood. But Nate and Joe and Gary and I are, are still, are still at it, and Nate's condition seems, it seems like it's getting worse these days, Joe has had two new suits that were just about the same as his other suits but different colors, and Gary still has stains on his shirts that he makes into, into ephemeral art. Joe still has his two squirts of butter buttered popcorn although most places don't use real butter anymore, and I, I still have my Dots.

I still work at, at Wallichs Music City and so does, so does Nametag Walter and I've gotten three raises since 1968. Oh, and my new used 1965 Plymouth Belvedere Satellite has never, never given me any problems and someone just a few weeks ago came up to me when I was, when I was parking to go see a Major Studio Preview at the Village, and he, he asked if I wanted to sell the car and he said he'd pay $3,000 for it if I, if I wanted to but I didn't want to even though that was double what we paid for it.

I have dinner at, at mother and father's a lot and mother still goes to, goes to Major Studio Previews with me sometimes, although she thinks that too many movies are too racy for her taste but father always says the racier the better but he doesn't go to the movies anymore because he, because he can't keep his eyes open for more than ten minutes and he doesn't think it's good to pay, to pay money to see a movie that you sleep through and besides, he doesn't, he doesn't need to spend that money with the prices they're charging for movies now because that would put him in the poorhouse.

I guess, I guess I should say that I'm thirty-four now and I'm still 5'3" small and I still, I still wear my Hollywood Stars baseball cap and it's still hanging on, just like, just like me. Mother washes it carefully and takes good care of it.

That brings us, that brings us up to date, I think. So, I want to, I want to talk about what just happened because it was so interesting and so I thought I'd, I'd talk about it on this cassette machine, you know, just to have a record of it. So, here's what just happened, but we, we have to go back to last month first. Oh, it's June 21st when I'm, when I'm making this record on cassette.

Anyway, last month the Paramount man, who still worked at Paramount, he, he called and asked if I, if I wanted to see a sneak preview of a new Paramount movie and that he really wanted me to see it and I also might enjoy the little trip that I'd be, that I'd be taking. That part seemed weird to me because I'd never, I'd never taken a trip anywhere in my, in my entire life and why would I need to, why would I need to take a trip to see a Major Studio Preview?

So, I said I didn't know what the trip part meant so he told me that the, that the preview was in San Luis Obispo and that, that sounded like a name Jerry Lewis would say in a movie. I didn't know where San Luis Obispo was and the Paramount man told me it was near Santa Barbara at a big theater there called the Fremont and it was, it was a really important picture for Paramount and they didn't want to preview it in Los Angeles because, because a couple of people at the, at the studio were worried about something to do with the picture and so they wanted to preview it away from Los Angeles.

He said he wanted to know what I thought because he always thought my opinions were, were worth hearing. I said I didn't, I didn't know where Santa Barbara was either and he said it was a three-hour drive and I, I said I'd never driven anywhere that far and he said I didn't have to drive, that they'd send a car to pick me up and then they'd drive me back as soon as the preview ended. I'd never, I'd never been picked up and driven anywhere by anyone other than mother, so that seemed good that I'd be picked up and driven so I said of course I'd come but I'd, I'd have to make arrangements at Wallichs Music City if it was a weekday. He said it was on a Saturday so that was fine because I didn't work on Saturday or Sunday usually. He said great, that the preview was in two days, on May 4th.

So, a Paramount car came and picked me up at 3:30 and it was a, a big car like I'd never seen and I, I sat in the back of it and the, the driver opened the door for me and everything and he, he wore a hat too, but not like a Hollywood Stars baseball cap, but more like a hat like a policeman would wear even though he wasn't a, wasn't a policeman. It was interesting to be in a big car sitting in the back with a driver driving me. It was a very long drive but I, I enjoyed looking out the window at things.

Anyway, we finally got there and it, it felt so good to get out of the big car and stretch my, my legs, although there wasn't much to stretch. I asked the driver what time it was and he said 6:30. So, he, he took me inside the Fremont Theater, which was a very nice big theater and he said to please wait in the lobby and he'd, he'd find the Paramount man for me. He came back and said the Paramount man would be there at around 7:00 and that I could, I could wait in the lobby or go watch the rest of the movie that was playing, which was *The Sting*, but I, I hadn't seen that movie yet and I, I didn't want to come in in the middle of it.

So, I used the men's room and then, and then sat in the lobby. The preview was starting at 8:00. The Paramount man got there at 7:00 and saw me sitting and came up to me and said he hoped the ride was fine and I said it was long but fine and I enjoyed it. He said to just go in the theater after *The Sting* was done and that he'd, that he'd find me after the movie, and then he went and talked to other people. I went to the, to the candy counter and bought my Dots, then at 7:15 *The Sting* let out so I, I went in and got my, my good seat and of course none of the other preview nuts were there because I was in San Luis Obispo and they didn't even, even know about this Major Studio Preview or that I was, that I was invited to it.

Anyway, the theater was full and the movie started right at 8:00 and I already knew it was a Paramount picture. The titles came on and said Jack Nicholson and Faye Dunaway in *Chinatown* and I'd seen Jack Nicholson in a couple of movies and I, I liked him, and I liked Faye Dunaway from *Bonnie and Clyde*, so that was good. The music was, the music was kind of weird and so I thought it might be a scary movie but then it changed to something not as weird but it was still weird. The last title was Directed by Roman Polanski and I, I liked his movies because of *Repulsion* and *Rosemary's Baby*, which I saw at the Crest when I was seeing another Major Studio Preview and *Rosemary's Baby* was one of my favorites.

The story was interesting but I had to, I had to really pay attention so I wouldn't get confused, and I liked all the actors and it was moody and there was one scene that I didn't understand at all where Faye Dunaway kept saying a young girl was her sister then Jack Nicholson would, would slap her and she'd say the girl was her, her daughter and he'd slap her again and she'd say my sister and he'd slap her again and she'd say my daughter and then it's my sister *and* my daughter, do I have to draw you a picture and I wish she'd draw *me* a picture because that was weird and I didn't really understand it but later I did because mother explained it to me.

Oh, and there was another scene where some short guy like, like me sliced Jack Nicholson's nose with a knife and that was, that was disturbing with lots of blood spurting everywhere and then he, he had a big bandage on his nose for a while. Anyway, nothing turns out good for, for anyone and then it ends with a line, "Forget it, Jake, it's Chinatown" and I thought that was a good line to end the movie and I really liked the movie quite a lot except not the music, which, well, just didn't, it just didn't seem to, to go with the movie at all.

After the movie, I went to the lobby and I could, I could see a lot of people huddled together, talking and gesturing and it, it didn't look like they were, like they were too happy. Then the Paramount man came over to me and said what did you think, be honest. I said I, I really liked the movie and the actors and the story even though it, it wasn't a happy story, and I liked everything but I thought the music was kind of weird. He said why? I said I wasn't sure how to, how to explain it but that it didn't, it didn't seem like it fit the movie and that it was weird sounding sometimes and it just, it just didn't, well, I didn't know how to, how to describe it better. He said you're describing it very well and I want you to describe it to the producer of the movie the way you just described it to me. He said wait here so I waited here.

Then he came back with a man, I guess the producer of the movie, and he was the, he was the tannest man I'd ever seen, like he'd been in the, in the sun for a, for a year. The Paramount man said, Bob Evans this is Preview Harvey and he goes to a lot of previews every year and we've come to appreciate his comments and I think you'll be interested in what he has to say. Bob Evans looked at me and said I've heard about you and yes, tell me what you thought of the picture, I'm genuinely interested. I repeated the same thing I told the Paramount man and Mr. Evans listened to me and when I was, when I was done he said I've got to tell you, I agree with you 110 percent about the music and I've been telling everyone that for weeks. He said but we're all so close to the movie so it's nice to hear it from a regular audience member and I appreciate your coming to see the picture and your comments.

Mr. Evans shook my hand and walked back to his group, talking and gesturing like before, and I guess, I guess that was that and the Paramount man thanked me for coming and then I got driven home for three hours and didn't get home until, until almost two in the, in the morning and I'd never been up that late and I thought it was such an interesting adventure, being driven by someone to a Major Studio Preview in San Luis Obispo and then talking to the, talking to the actual producer of the movie, Mr. Evans, and I couldn't wait to tell mother all about it, but it was two in the morning so I didn't call her till the, till the real morning when I got up.

But that's not, that's not the end of the story. Here's the, here's the end of the story. *Chinatown* opened six weeks later, which is now, June 21st, in only two theaters, the Chinese in, in Hollywood and the National in Westwood. I haven't talked about the, the National because it wasn't there when I stopped making cassettes in 1968. It was built in, in 1970 and it was a, a very nice big theater but didn't, didn't feel like a real movie theater like the Chinese or the Village, so I went after work at Wallichs Music City to see *Chinatown* at the, at the Chinese and that felt right anyway because, well, you know, *Chinatown* the movie at the Chinese.

So, the movie starts and it's the same titles only the music, the music is completely different and very pretty and sad and haunting with a trumpet and it was, it was like watching a whole different movie and I thought that was interesting how different music could, could make such a big difference, but, but everything seemed easier to understand and it just made me love the movie, even though it was still disturbing sometimes. The new music was by Jerry Goldsmith and I loved his music from *A Patch of Blue* and *Seconds* and lots of other movies, although Henry Mancini was still my, my favorite.

Anyway, I just, I just wanted to make a record of that because it was interesting, and now I'll press the off button again.

Okay, I'm, I'm back because I wanted to, I wanted to make another record of something interesting that just happened and so here I am again and I'll try not to be too yakky but here's what was interesting that happened tonight. Oh, tonight is Friday, August 8th, 1975 and I, I just got home from a Sneak Preview at a theater I'd, I'd never been to in Pasadena and I'd never been to Pasadena either and I got so lost trying to, trying to find the theater but finally a gas station man wrote down exactly how to get there so I, so I finally got there. The name of the theater was the Academy.

But here's why I went. I went because a man from Mann Theaters called me on the, on the telephone and said he'd gotten my number from Blake Edwards, that he knew Blake Edwards and that he knew who I was because he, he worked for Mann Theaters and they owned a lot of movie theaters where I saw Major Studio Previews including the Village so he knew all about me and that I was known as Preview Harvey and that Mr. Edwards called me his, his good luck charm.

Anyway, the Mann Theaters man said a friend of his had, had called him and asked if he, if he could find me and to let me know that this friend of his would like me to come to a Sneak Preview in Pasadena at the Academy Theater and that was a, that was a Mann Theater and the Mann Theater man had arranged the Sneak Preview. He said his friend told him it would mean a lot if I was there, but I didn't know who his friend was or why it would mean a lot but I, but I said of course I'd go. He told me they'd be showing a work print in interlock sound and I, I didn't know what that meant so he, he explained to me that a work print was the print that was used to edit the movie and so it was separate picture and sound and took two machines to run the film and I, I still wasn't sure I understood it, but he said the preview is at 8:30 and the regular film was *Tommy*, in case I wanted to see that. I didn't really want to see a movie called *Tommy* so I just, I just got there for the preview and got my Dots and a good seat. My other preview nuts were there but not Terrence because it was, it was probably too far from his high school to drive. But Nate and Joe and Gary were there and so was that, that other preview nut who always waved at me.

So, the theater is really big and it's almost full and the movie starts and it says something about like what the Mann Theaters man said, that it was a, a work print and would have scratches and marks and stuff and that some opticals like fade outs and fade ins and dissolves wouldn't be there, and I, I thought that was interesting.

Anyway, the movie starts and the work print is pretty scratchy and all that, but the movie is, is really funny and maybe the raciest thing I've ever seen, with so many naked people where you saw everything, women and men, and I mean, I mean all the time, all their naked parts, but it was all funny, not dirty and the audience was laughing really hard at everything. There was one scene where the two, the two people in front of me were laughing so hard that they were, they were stomping their feet on the floor.

But that wasn't the interesting thing. The interesting thing was that one of the three main people in the picture, who was also the writer and the, and the co-director, and I'd never seen that title before, co-director, but the minute he came on screen twenty minutes into the movie, it was, it was that guy, that guy, the preview nut who always waved at me at all those Major Studio Previews for so many years, it was that same guy and he'd waved at me again just before the movie started. I just, I just couldn't believe that a preview nut made a movie and I was, I was seeing it because he wanted me to be at the Sneak Preview.

After the movie, I, I went up the aisle and he was standing there with, with other people, including the girl from the movie who I'd seen in other movies and he, he looked up and saw me and I said you made a movie and it was funny and I can't believe you made a movie and he said Preview Harvey, you being here means so much to me, because this is my first movie and it only feels real and like I've arrived because Preview Harvey is here. I've been seeing you at previews since I was fifteen years old. It wouldn't have been the same if you weren't here.

He introduced me to the, to the Mann Theaters man and his name was Geoffrey Berkman and, and I introduced him to, to Nate and Joe and Gary, who'd come over to, to see what was going on. Anyway, I, I went home and didn't get lost this time and called mother and told her I'd just seen a Sneak Preview in Pasadena and that the man who made the movie was a fellow preview nut who always waved at me since he was fifteen and used to always see me at Major Studio Previews. She thought that was an amazing thing and I did, I did too. She asked if we could see the movie whenever it came out but I, I told her there were a lot of naked people and that you, that you saw all their naked parts and all the time but that it was funny but she said it sounded like it wasn't for her because of all the, all the naked people and the naked parts all the time. Anyway, I thought I should, I should make a record of tonight because it was so interesting that I finally met the fellow preview nut who'd waved at me at all those Major Studio Previews and had made a movie.

Okay, I guess that's, that's it and I'm pushing the off button now.

Okay, I guess, I guess I should make a record even though I don't, I don't really want to, I guess I should but it's a sad record and I don't know how to, I don't know how to even say it. Nametag Walter died. He, he hadn't been to work in a couple of months, but before that he, he told me he had some kind of, some kind of cancer thing and it was, it wasn't good and he looked really bad and I was, I was worried about him and then he stopped coming to work and this morning they told me he died and I, and I just went and sat by myself and didn't know what to do. I don't know if he was, if he was my friend, but he always seemed like he was and he was, he was always so kind to me and always told me I was his best employee and all that stuff he said. They told me he was, he was only sixty, and that was, that was too young to be dead already. They said I could go home early if I wanted to but I didn't want to because I worked until five and I felt I should be there until five like I always was with Nametag Walter.

I called mother when I got home and she told me how sad it was and she said I sounded sad and that it was, it was okay to cry if I needed to cry and I, I guess I needed to cry because I put on the *Soldier in the Rain* music and cried all night and then decided to make this record since there's plenty of room on this, on this cassette. I guess I should say it's March 10th, 1977. I have to push the off button now.

Okay, I'm back again and I guess I need to make another record. It's 1978 and I just had my last day at Wallichs Music City because they closed the store and it's, and it's going to be torn down next week. I feel like it was my, my third home after my studio or efficiency apartment and mother and father's house on Rexford in fake Beverly Hills. I've been working at Wallichs Music City for twenty years, that's a, that's a long time and now that's done and I'm, I'm not sure what to do.

Wallichs Music City hasn't been doing so well for the last six or seven years because of, because of Tower Records. All the people who used to come to Wallichs Music City stopped coming because that's what, that's what people seem to do when there's something new and they just move to that new place and don't even care about the place they'd been coming to for years, they just don't care about that place anymore and that's not right, at least I don't think it's right. There was no other record store like, like Wallichs Music City and I went to, I went to Tower Records once and it just wasn't as nice and it didn't have as many things as Wallichs Music City had. Mother was sad too, but she said time marches on and I said I wish time would stop marching on already and just, and just leave the nice things alone. She said you'll be okay, you'll find something else but I didn't think I'd ever find anything else like Wallichs Music City, I just didn't.

It's good that I, that I have a nice amount of money in the bank because other than, than movies and food I never spent it on anything, so I don't have to worry for a while, and so I won't worry for a while. Anyway, I still have my Major Studio Previews and that's the, that's the most important thing. Anyway, that's the record I wanted to make and I'll push the off button now.

I guess, I guess I'm back and I think this will be the, the last record I make on cassettes. It's 1981 and somehow, I don't know how, really, and mother doesn't know how, really, but I'm forty-one now. I don't, I don't really feel any different than before but I'm forty-one now and it's 1981 and I think, I think, well, I think the world has changed so much that I don't even know which side is up and which side is down anymore. I don't like change, not the, not the kind of change of the last few years, not that kind of change, like Nametag Walter dying or Wallichs Music City closing and I, I made a record of that, and not the kind of change like them tearing Wallichs Music

City down and putting up a, I don't even know what they call it but it was ugly and had a few stores in it and mother called it a strip mall but I didn't know what that meant and to me, it was, it was just an ugly thing with stores and a parking lot.

Anyway, I haven't worked since Wallichs Music City closed, I just, I just didn't know where I'd work and I had enough money saved to not worry about it as long as I, as long as I didn't spend too much and not spending too much became simple and that's because of the other change, the big change that, that, well, that changed everything. I, I noticed it happening in 1978 and more in 1979, when the way they did Major Studio Previews began changing and, and none of us preview nuts were happy about it.

They, they began telling you who was in the Major Studio Preview and then they just began telling you what the Major Studio Preview was, I mean, the title of the movie, and that wasn't a Major Studio Preview at all and none of the studio people who knew me were going anymore and no one cared about Preview Harvey or his, or his opinions anymore and so my fellow preview nuts and I stopped caring and stopped going to Major Studio Previews.

Oh, every once in a while there'd be a Major Studio Preview that was a secret and we went to those, but it just wasn't the same and one by one, first Nate, whose condition was so bad he could barely sit through a movie anymore, then Joe, then Gary, they all stopped going. Terrence had stopped before then because he was, he was a successful teacher and too busy and I guess I held out the, the longest but I, I finally gave up too and just as well because, because now in the year 1981 there aren't any Major Studio Previews at all, they, they just don't, they don't do them anymore.

So, I wasn't a preview nut anymore because everything had changed and there was no Wallichs Music City, no friends, just mother and father and I guess I have no life because I have no Major Studio Previews and that may, that may sound weird but, but that *was* my life, that's what I, what I lived for, that's all I cared about, all I thought about, and all I, all I really needed.

But wasn't it, wasn't it the most amazing time? It was and I was there and I was Preview Harvey and I was part of it. Sometimes I, I think about what if I hadn't been Preview Harvey, what if I hadn't been 5'3" small and balding and wearing a Hollywood Stars baseball cap and fixated on Major Studio Previews and hadn't had my, my That's Just Harvey condition?

It's, it's like that movie I saw once, *Seconds*, where people got a, a second chance at life and could come back like Rock Hudson and what if I came back like Rock Hudson with hair and taller and what if I didn't have a That's Just Harvey condition, what would, what would that have been like? But I don't know what, what any of that would have, would have been like because *Seconds* was just a movie and you can't get a second chance at life and come back as Rock Hudson because I think we're, we're who we're supposed to be and I was supposed to be Preview Harvey and I had a purpose and value and worth and all those studio men said I had good movie sense and Jerry Lewis gave me my nickname and Blake Edwards said I was his good luck charm and he wanted the Preview Harvey seal of approval, and I had fellow preview nut people I cared about and I saw so many wonderful Major Studio Previews and all that, all that has to count for something, right?

Anyway, sorry for being a motormouth and yakky but I just, I just wanted to make one final record of things on cassette and now I'm pushing the off button for good and putting the cassette machine away because I, I don't really have anything else to say.

POSTSCRIPT

Harvey Minton, aka Preview Harvey, passed away in 1983 of what they called natural causes. I think the real cause of death was that he had no purpose anymore, nothing to live for. I think he just went to bed one night and died because there was nothing else for him to do.

Well, as he would have said, and I think it's just how I'll close this book: That's Just Harvey.

N.G.
Ladera Ranch, California
March 2023

ACKNOWLEDGEMENTS

As always, none of the twenty-three books I've written would be what they are without my muse, Margaret Willock Jones. Many thanks to my two eagle-eyed proofers, John Griffin and Charles Smith; cover designer, Doug Haverty; Marc Wanamaker of Bison Archives for the amazing cover photo; and my Darling Daughter, Jennifer.

I got the idea for this book almost twenty years ago but could never figure out how to write it until December of 2022, when it all came to me as Preview Harvey would say, out of the blue. Whilc thc book is a complete work of fiction, the character of Preview Harvey was inspired by a real-life person who was a staple at Major Studio Previews, as was I. It really was an amazing time and I had great fun revisiting it and bathing in the glow of old movie theaters, giant screens, Cinemascope, VistaVision, Technicolor, and a time before smartphones, Alexa, smart TVs, the internet, and social media. I encourage everyone to check out the addendum that follows, a list of every preview mentioned in this book. They're all worth seeking out, even the stinkers.

THE MOVIES

Hold That Blonde
The High and the Mighty
Target Earth
Bad Day at Black Rock
Mister Roberts
To Catch a Thief
How to Be Very, Very Popular
The Tender Trap
Bus Stop
The Girl Can't Help It
The Wayward Bus
Hollywood or Bust
The Killing
Bernardine
Desk Set
The Spirit of St. Louis
Will Success Spoil Rock Hunter?

Bell, Book and Candle
The Fly
Some Came Running
Vertigo
Auntie Mame
Anatomy of a Murder
Some Like It Hot
A Hole in the Head
Journey to the Center of the Earth
Rio Bravo
Visit to a Small Planet
Come Dance with Me
A Summer Place
Blue Denim
Fade In
The Bellboy
The Rat Race
High Time
The Crowded Sky
Midnight Lace
Strangers When We Meet
The Subterraneans
Village of the Damned
Voyage to the Bottom of the Sea
Fanny
The Great Impostor
The Last Time I Saw Archie
One-Eyed Jacks
Wild in the Country
The Naked Edge
Breakfast at Tiffany's
Bachelor Flat
Light in the Piazza

The Road to Hong Kong
Experiment in Terror
I Thank a Fool
The Man Who Shot Liberty Valance
Mr. Hobbs Takes a Vacation
Requiem for a Heavyweight
Pressure Point
The Manchurian Candidate
Days of Wine and Roses
If a Man Answers
David and Lisa
The Trial
Sundays and Cybele
The Courtship of Eddie's Father
Papa's Delicate Condition
Call Me Bwana
My Six Loves
The Man from the Diners' Club
The List of Adrian Messenger
The Nutty Professor
The Great Escape
Toys in the Attic
The Caretakers
Lilies of the Field
Under the Yum Yum Tree
Mary, Mary
Lord of the Flies
Soldier in the Rain
Charade
The Prize
Kings of the Sun
The Comedy of Terrors
Ladybug Ladybug

The Pink Panther
Dr. Strangelove or: How I Stopped Worrying and Learned to Love the Bomb
The Third Secret
Girl With Green Eyes
Honeymoon Hotel
Woman of Straw
The Unsinkable Molly Brown
Fail Safe
That Man from Rio
Dear Heart
Goldfinger
36 Hours
Strange Bedfellows
The Umbrellas of Cherbourg
How to Murder Your Wife
The Amorous Adventures of Moll Flanders
Mirage
What's New Pussycat?
Inside Daisy Clover
The Sandpiper
The Reward
Repulsion
A Patch of Blue
Harper
Lord Love a Duck
The Fortune Cookie
The Singing Nun
Torn Curtain
The Trouble with Angels
Fantastic Voyage
Big Hand for a Little Lady
Gambit

Seconds
The Professionals
You're a Big Boy Now
Hotel
Oh Dad, Poor Dad, Mamma's Hung You in the Closet and I'm Feelin' So Sad
How to Succeed in Business Without Really Trying
The Family Way
The Dirty Dozen
Bonnie and Clyde
Up the Down Staircase
Wait Until Dark
The Party
Chinatown
And, of course, the unnamed movie is *The First Nudie Musical*